INTO THE LYON'S DEN

The Lyon's Den Connected World

Jade Lee

ARE YOU SIGNED UP FOR DRAGONBLADE'S BLOG?

You'll get the latest news and information on exclusive giveaways, exclusive excerpts, coming releases, sales, free books, cover reveals and more.

Check out our complete list of authors, too!

No spam, no junk. That's a promise!

Sign Up Here

www.dragonbladepublishing.com

Dearest Reader;

Thank you for your support of a small press. At Dragonblade Publishing, we strive to bring you the highest quality Historical Romance from the some of the best authors in the business. Without your support, there is no 'us', so we sincerely hope you adore these stories and find some new favorite authors along the way.

Happy Reading!

CEO, Dragonblade Publishing

Additional Dragonblade books by Author Jade Lee

The Lyon's Den Connected World
Into the Lyon's Den

*** Please visit Dragonblade's website for a full list of books and authors. Sign up for Dragonblade's blog for sneak peeks, interviews, and more: ***
www.dragonbladepublishing.com

CHAPTER ONE

A MBER GOLD WAS dancing with the Prince of Wales when the summons came. She pretended she hadn't heard it. She was at the most glorious ball and would not be distracted. Especially since her partner was not the old, fat prince, but an imaginary royal who had a laugh that brought colors to her mind, such as could not be imagined on this mortal Earth.

He was, needless to say, an exceptional prince and thoroughly devoted to her.

"Quit yer lollygagging!" Hippolyta grumbled. She was the pit boss in this gambling den and in charge of all the dealers. Also, she despised anyone who sat still for more than five seconds. "The Lyon wants to see you now, and with your best manners, no less."

"Go, girl," her grandfather said. Hippolyta had woken him from his doze.

Amber stood, shaking out her dull gray skirt in the equally dull light from a single lantern. The cage room of the Lyon's Den gambling house was cramped and noisy, but most of all, to Amber's eyes, it was boring. Dark wood, dingy paper on the walls (if it had ever been papered), and a window with no curtains. Even the night sky was muted, covered in London's perpetual fog.

She pulled the cage door open, nodding briefly to the Abacas Woman, who sat with her and her grandfather. Then she walked quickly along the walls of the main floor. She knew all the workers here from the injured soldiers who guarded the doors, the pretty, boy dealers who smiled often, and most especially the girls who worked upstairs or down. Of course, she did. She spent every horrible hour of every evening here until her eyes burned from the smoke, and she despised the sound of men's laughter.

Knocking twice on the door to Mrs. Dove-Lyon's private parlor, she was quickly bid to enter.

She stepped inside, keeping her hands tucked neatly together while her scarf obscured most of her face. The proprietress stayed seated at her tea table with a cup in hand. Across from her reclined a man Amber disliked immediately for his somber attire. All in black except a diamond stickpin piercing straight through his white cravat.

Why would anyone—man, woman, or child—wear black when there was a world of colors available? He was clearly not a man of the cloth, though he had never come into the Den before as far as she could remember. He was wealthy because his jacket was of the highest quality and quite fashionable, but it was also drab, and today she despised dull above all things. Would she never escape her very black and gray life?

"How may I serve?" she asked, keeping her voice modest though the words stuck in her throat. She was not an employee like the others. She was an extension of her family's jewelry business. Whatever arrangement this man and the Lyon had did not involve giving her any coins at all.

"Thisbe, welcome," Mrs. Dove-Lyon said in a soft voice. She referred to Amber by the name of a character in *A Midsummer Night's Dream*. All the workers in the Den had a character's name except Amber, who had been given the name from the play within the play.

Stupid and annoying, but such was the shadow part she played in this place. "Let me introduce you to Lord Byrn. He has come here with a very specific request."

She'd just bet he had. It was the somber ones who wished for the oddest things. But given that she was not one of the upstairs girls, she had no idea what any of that would have to do with her. Still, she had to be polite. "My lord?"

"A young man came here a month ago, Mr. Laurence John. His father is Lord Morthan."

She remembered him well by the clashing colors of his waistcoat. Which, come to think of it, she still preferred to Lord Byrn's attire.

"He sold a brooch to your grandfather. Heavy gold, a single blood-red ruby surrounded by eight diamonds."

It had been seven diamonds as one had gone missing, and the piece had been filthy beyond belief. It had been a joy to see the original gemstones revealed once she'd cleaned it and melted down the gold. Either way, they were not in the habit of discussing what had been bought or sold or remade into something much more spectacular. She gave a delicate shrug.

"If you say so, my lord, but there is no such piece in my family's collection now. There is, however, a large selection of brooches in the Dragon's Hoard." The store sat at the corner of this building, just below the den. It made for easy and secure movement of jewelry pawned by the Den's customers. "If you would go downstairs—"

"I have already been there," he interrupted. "There are no rubies below, such as I describe."

Because the rare gem was locked up in the depths of the store where she intended to fashion it as the heart of a bird in flight. She had sculpted the wax yesterday, and her father declared it the most beautiful piece she'd ever done. But already, she could see that her dream was about to be destroyed. If this lord wished a ruby for a different reason, then money would certainly trump art.

"Have you spoken with my father?" she asked, finding it hard to keep her smile in place. "Perhaps he can design what you wish."

"I have spoken with him." Lord Byrn leaned forward in his chair. "He said to discuss matters with you."

Never. Her father and grandfather had dedicated their lives to keeping her talents hidden. They claimed it was to keep her respectable since women did not fashion jewelry. She thought it was so they could sell her designs and keep all the praise—and profits—for themselves. But she couldn't say that aloud. Instead, she pulled on her most addlepated tone, pitching her voice high and stupid.

"I cannot fathom why my father would say such a thing."

"Perhaps because it is you who have the piece." He smiled. "I have seen your grandfather. His eyes are rheumy, and his hands shake. He sleeps most of the evenings here except when you rouse him to tell him what to say about some gemstone or another. You are the fence here, and it does you no credit to claim otherwise."

Amber rocked back on her heels, surprised that any man had seen so much. Her grandfather was kept in the back in the dark, so none would see his condition. They had taken as many pains with her grandfather's weakness as they had to hide her talent. But before she could think of an appropriate response, Lord Byrn pressed his point with a voice that was surprisingly compelling.

"I have seen you take walks with him in the afternoon," he said in a gentle tone. "You look a pretty pair, and there is genuine love between you."

"Of course, there is!" she said. "He's my grandfather."

"Even so," he said, dipping his chin in agreement. "But if he was capable of creating such pieces as are sold below, that time has long since passed."

He had been an artist of great renown, once upon a time. And the family name—the original name of Gohar—still had a fine reputation on the continent. But not here where they were known simply as the

Gold family, selling jewelry beneath a disreputable gaming hell.

"I need that brooch, Miss Gold," he said, his voice growing stronger. "I don't care why you have hidden it from your family, but that piece was not his to sell. It belongs to the dowager countess, and she has a great deal of influence among the elite. If you—and Mrs. Dove-Lyon—wish to keep your business dealings private, then I suggest you return it to me now. Otherwise, I cannot answer to what she will do. Her granddaughter is to be presented at court in a few weeks' time, and every female Morthan has worn that brooch during their presentation since the time of William the Conqueror."

Well, hell, that was trouble for sure. But they were not in the habit of returning purchases. Certainly not without an offer of significant recompense. So, she raised her hands in a helpless gesture. "Unfortunately, I cannot make something appear that we do not have. Perhaps the dowager countess merely misplaced it. After all, if it is hers, then how would her grandson have gotten hold of it to sell to us?" A reasonable, logical answer, except this man knew better.

"You and I both know the answer. Larry is a light-fingered fool. He stole it and gambled it away here."

She shook her head. "I do not remember him, my lord." A bald-faced lie.

"That will not make a difference when the constable comes knocking."

"The constable!" Mrs. Dove-Lyon exclaimed. "Really, Lord Byrn, threats do you no credit. Perhaps we can come to some arrangement. You say the dowager countess has lost her brooch? Well, the Gold family can fashion a brooch, can they not?"

Amber smiled sweetly, knowing that unlike the light-fingered Larry, Lord Byrn appeared to have a great deal of ready blunt. "Of course, we can. What sort of design—"

"The original design," he snapped, clearly frustrated with the conversation so far. "The original brooch."

"Which we do not have," Amber said, her voice matching his in tone. "So, either commission a new one, or I need to return to my grandfather." She shot Lord Byrn an ugly look. "It is time for his special tea. The one from China that clears his sight and steadies his hands for the work he loves to do."

She was about to turn away when his expression shifted. Instead of the imperious lord, he softened into a charming scapegrace. He laughed in a light kind of desperation and reached out with long, elegant fingers. Fingers, she noted with surprise, that sported callouses. "Please, please, you must forgive my frustration. This has been a difficult task for a family that is not even my own."

That was true, which brought her to the obvious question. "Why does it fall to you?"

"I am sponsoring a resolution in the House of Lords to help our wounded veterans. As you know, so many have come from Waterloo, a shadow of their former selves. They have nothing but the clothes on their backs and nightmares that plague them. Surely you know this." He turned to Mrs. Dove-Lyon. "You yourself have done good work in hiring the military men. They guard your doors with skill, but there are so many more that need help."

Very true. The stories she had heard from the dozen who guarded their den were terrifying enough. "But what has that to do with the countess's brooch?"

"Her son, Lord Morthan, will vote with me if I return the missing brooch."

Mrs. Dove-Lyon sniffed. "You cannot appeal to his sense of duty? To his patriotism? It is only fitting that the Crown help those who have given so much for our own defense!"

"I agree!" Lord Byrn said. The passion was clear in his voice. "That is why I am working so tirelessly to accomplish what must be done. For our wounded soldiers who have given so much."

"Yes, of course," said Mrs. Dove-Lyon. "Quite proper."

Well, he had the Lyon eating out of his hands. And if there was any doubt, the woman then turned to Amber with a pleading expression. "Can you think of no way to help, Thisbe?" she pressed.

"I cannot sell what I do not have. The brooch is not here."

"But it was here," Lord Byrn pressed. "Larry did sell it to you."

She could not admit the truth. Aristocrats did not like to be thwarted, and he would like it even less to find out that the piece had been melted for parts.

"I don't have it," she repeated, investing her words with the absolute truth.

"Then who does?" asked Mrs. Dove-Lyon.

Amber winced. It was one thing to ignore his lordship. He would likely never grace the Den again. But Mrs. Dove-Lyon carried their lease for the store below and their position inside the Den. She had the ability to toss them out at her whim. Plus, she already knew that Mr. Laurence John had sold the piece to them. Which meant she likely guessed what had happened. She made that very clear in the next moment as she set down her teacup with an audible click.

"I wish to help Lord Byrn," declared Mrs. Dove-Lyon. "I have heard much of his political influence. His resolution would help a great many people."

Amber sighed. She had no choice but to tell the truth now. Mrs. Dove-Lyon did not often give aid, but when she did, she expected others to comply. Amber grit her teeth and met Lord Byrn's gaze.

"The piece is gone, my lord. It did come to us, but is now gone."

"Sold to whom? Who would purchase such a thing?"

She would. To melt it down and make something beautiful out of an old, crusty ornament, so clearly unloved.

"No one purchased it," she bit out. "It was melted down last week. I have only the main stone, and a bit of gold left. The rest went into other pieces." She added a last part because she was angry. "And there were only seven diamonds. The eighth had gone missing."

"Then why did you lie about it? You said you never came by it."
He didn't sound angry so much as curious.

"Because I do not have what you want, and if I told you the truth,
you would demand recompense. Mr. John sold the brooch to us and
was paid a fair price for it. But you would demand the gemstones back,
and you would threaten the constable or worse, all because a foolish
boy sold something that did not belong to him. That is not our fault,
my lord. And we cannot willy nilly return jewelry to every nob who
sold something that did not belong to him merely because he wants
it."

Though they were a legitimate business—the buying and selling of
jewelry—a single, angry aristocrat could bring it all down. It was, in
fact, why they had left Germany so long ago. A wastrel prince had
made them fear for their lives. They had run here to England, called
themselves Gold, and set up beneath a gambling den. And any hope of
respectability for their daughter disappeared the moment they opened
up shop. The English did not wed nobody foreigners who worked in a
den.

"So, you lie?" he asked.

"Yes. Because gentlemen like you do not like being told no. Much
better to say, I know nothing about what you speak. Nothing at all."

He grunted in acknowledgment. "Yes, I suppose that is the wiser
course."

Amber gaped at him. She had not expected him to be so reasonable. But she wasn't about to look a gift horse in the mouth. She smiled,
curtsied, and rushed her next words. "If there is nothing else—"

"Could you fashion it again? I could pay you for your work, of
course. A reasonable sum. You have the gemstones, you said."

"Of course, she can," Mrs. Dove-Lyon said. "Thisbe is a genius
with jewelry. She has created the most magical pieces, my lord. Simply
magical."

"No!" Amber cried out. "I can't!"

Lord Byrn's expression was surprised, but it was Mrs. Dove-Lyon's face that made Amber pause. It was hard and angry. This was the Lyon's face, the one that forced men's hands, making them wed where they did not will it. The one that had become infamous throughout London. "But, of course, you can, Thisbe. Because that is why you are here. Unless I should speak with another jeweler. There have been so many lately asking to rent the space where your family's shop resides. Perhaps it's time I revisited the terms of your lease."

It was a real threat. Any jeweler in town would be thrilled to set up here to buy gems from desperate gamblers. And if her family was unceremoniously tossed out, there was nowhere else for them to establish themselves. It had been a godsend that they found the Lyon's Den.

"I am, of course, willing to try," Amber amended hastily. "But I do not remember the design." She looked at Lord Byrn. "Do you have a sketch of it?"

His hands lifted in a gesture of confusion. "Only the description I gave you. A blood-red ruby and eight diamonds."

"Seven," she corrected. "And that is not enough if you want me to recreate a brooch to match a set from the time of William the Conqueror."

Lord Byrn blew out a breath as he stared at her. His expression was heavy, and his...well, his eyes were quite lovely. She hadn't noticed it before now, but they were the most striking shade of green with just enough blue to make them the color of the rarest form of emerald. They startled her enough to cut off her breath and words.

"Could you do it from a painting, perhaps?" he asked.

She frowned. "If it were a good painting."

"The very best, I'm told." He nodded as if that decided it. "I shall come for you tomorrow at three. I'll say you are a cousin or something from the Continent with an interest in portraiture. That should gain us admittance. The family is quite proud of the damned thing."

She blinked. "What thing?"

"The portrait of the dowager countess wearing the brooch back when she was first presented at Court. Painted by Joseph Wright of Derby. He's quite famous."

She nodded. Even she had heard of the man. But painting faces and painting jewelry were two different things. Still, she had no room to argue, though she searched and searched her thoughts for a reason. Mrs. Dove-Lyon had no such reservations.

"Excellent, my lord. She shall be ready. We shall await you at the Dragon's Hoard."

CHAPTER TWO

E LLIOTT REES, EARL of Byrn, opened his eyes to a room flooded with sunlight and a screeching headache. As usual, that headache was called *Mother.*

"Good morning, Mother," he groaned.

"Morning! It's one of the clock in the afternoon!"

Of course, it was. After he'd left the Lyon's Den, he'd moved on to two other dens in the vicinity and connected with his wilder set of acquaintances. The drink had been plentiful, the gambling even more so, and he had managed to gather several useful tidbits about the peerage and their charges. The best information was that Lord Carderby's youngest son had been sent down from Harrow for creating a secret language and teaching it to his friends. Since they were boys, the pack had become obnoxious with their game and had been disciplined.

However, young Peter clearly demonstrated an exceptional mind and a talent for codes that the Home Office would find very useful one day. Elliott had recorded that note and several others before leaving the paper on the writing desk near the window. He now saw with approval that his secretary had taken the missives while Elliott slept and would already have them recorded and filed in the appropriate categories for later reference.

Unfortunately, none of that made the least difference to his mother.

"You promised, Elliott. You said you would attend luncheon at the Smitherbees' home. You expressed an interest in meeting their youngest daughter."

He had not. In fact, he already knew that Ada Smitherbees and her mother had an unfortunate interest in gambling. He'd noted that last night when her carriage had been waiting outside the ladies' entrance to the Lyon's Den. A quick chat and a shared bit of tobacco with the coachman had told him more than he wanted to know about the Smitherbees.

"Now get up, Elliott. We will leave in—"

"She gambles, Mother."

"Don't be ridiculous. All ladies gamble. Why, even I..." Her voice trailed off as Elliott stared hard at her. Eventually, she deflated. "How badly? You know I went to school with her mother."

He remembered. He always remembered details like that. "The mother has lost thousands of pounds this year alone. The daughter shows every sign of continuing the tradition."

His mother took the news with her usual dramatic flair. She slumped against his bedpost and set her palm to her forehead as if checking for a fever. "You're sure?" she said in a feeble tone.

He didn't respond because he knew he didn't need to. Plus, his head ached abominably.

"Of course, you're sure," she muttered. "And you're always right." She lowered her hand and glared at him. "But you have to marry someone. I work my fingers to the bone, trying to find you an appropriate wife, and you always find some excuse."

A gambling habit was not a petty excuse. The Smitherbees could lose a few thousand pounds a year without a blink. Elliott's family could not. And though their finances were immeasurably better since he'd taken the reins, they were not buried in blunt like so many of his mother's friends.

"You have to marry, Elliott, and soon. If you won't do it for an heir, then do it for Gwen's sake. Your sister needs a married woman to get her out of those books. Someone who can take her to parties and introduce her to an appropriate husband."

"Someone like Lord Dunnamore?"

His mother huffed out a breath. "Will you cease prattling to me about Lord Dunnamore? You don't remember what it was like after your father died. I was terrified, I tell you. *Terrified.* And Lord Dunnamore was one of your father's oldest friends."

Old was the significant word. His sister Diana had been seventeen. Lord Dunnamore had been nearing sixty with grown children of his own. And Elliott had been in school, so he hadn't known to object. Hell, he hadn't known anything except his own grief.

And so, Diana was married off to a man three times her age as a sacrifice to his mother's fear. That was bad enough, but then Lord Dunnamore had mismanaged their family finances until Elliott came of age. His other sister, Gwen, had retreated into her books and never come out. If it weren't for the companionship of his father's by-blow, Lilah, Gwen's voice would likely turn to rust from disuse.

All of which was to say that he did not think kindly of Lord Dunnamore, even more now that Diana was trapped in a sickroom with the elderly man. But his mother could never hear a word of criticism without hours of self-indulgent tears, so Elliott had found it easiest to spend as much time as possible away from her. Which was difficult given that she had barged into his bedroom without leave.

All these thoughts filtered through his mind while she continued to prattle on about the injustices of ungrateful children. In the end, Elliott settled for expediency.

"Mother, you are correct."

Naturally, she did not hear him the first time, so absorbed was she in her own words. Despite how it worsened his sore head, Elliott pitched his voice loud and hard. "Mother! You are correct!"

"Why I never." She blinked. "What did you say?"

"You are correct that it is high time I rose from my bed. I will not thank you for waking me. I had a long night—"

"I do not wish to hear what you were doing!"

Well, thank God for that since he had no intention of telling. "Pray, let me get up and dressed. I have an appointment."

"Yes. To luncheon with the Smitherbees. There must be some eligible lady—"

"No, Mother. I never said I'd go, as I am promised to walk with an entirely different lady."

If his head weren't throbbing, he wouldn't have made such a grievous error. Never would he have spoken of any lady at all, but he had, and now his mother pounced on the word as if it were a prize horse for her to examine before a race.

"What lady is this? Where is she from? Do I know her? How could you not tell me of this earlier? I insist on meeting her."

"She is not a marriage prospect," he said with some exasperation. "She is assisting me with a…a political matter."

"*Every* woman is a marriage prospect," she said with equal exasperation.

Now that was patently untrue. Except looking at his mother's face, he realized that she was indeed becoming desperate, though about what he couldn't fathom. Their finances were in decent shape, her health was good as was everyone else's in the household, and they were heading toward spring, the most robust time of the social season. She ought to be in a fine state, but something had turned her into a nervous woman who burst into his bedchamber unannounced.

"Mother, what is going on?"

She exhaled in a dramatic rush, then raised a handkerchief to her eye to wipe away a pretend tear. "You never listen!"

He had to give her that one. He'd ceased listening to her years ago. "Enlighten me, Mother. I am paying attention."

"You need to marry, so there is someone to help Gwendolyn!"

Off all the people in this house, Gwen was the most self-sufficient. Give her a book on some rare plant, and she was happy for days, if not weeks. "Lilah is here to give help and whatever companionship Gwen needs."

"A companion cannot make her attend parties! Or meet a husband! I have given up asking you to help."

Oh, good. It had only taken four years for that message to get through.

"—Diana cannot leave her husband's side."

More's the pity, and may the old bastard die soon. Diana will very much enjoy being a widow.

"—And so, it must be your wife, as Gwen will not listen to me. *Nobody* listens to me!"

He couldn't argue with her there, either. Only that she had created this very problem with her endless sense of dramatics.

Elliott rubbed a hand over his face, trying to focus his thoughts even as he scratched at his growing beard. "This has been true for years," he finally said as gently as he could. "Why the hysterics now?"

She glared at him with true hatred in her eyes. It was clear that his question was a grievous mistake, but he couldn't fathom why. In the end, he had to mollify her with an apology he didn't feel. "I am terribly sorry. I am feeling particularly obtuse this morning—er, today. Please explain this to me again?"

She rolled her eyes but obliged. "It is Gwen's birthday next month."

Yes, he knew. "I have specially arranged a visit to the royal botanical gardens for her as a present. She will—"

"Did you make sure there would be eligible bachelors there?"

Elliott frowned. "She despises eligible bachelors. Why would I give her a present she would despise?"

"Because she is turning nine and twenty! You cannot want to have an ape leader as a sister. Think of the humiliation."

As much as he knew that his mother was thinking of her own humiliation, Elliott had to acknowledge that she had yet another point. The title of spinster (he would not think the other insulting phrase) would not help his sister come out of her shell. Though she might appear to be content with her current, insular ways, he did believe she was lonely. And he did not like to think of her as unhappy, so he conceded his mother's point.

"I shall find someone suitable to join us at the royal gardens."

His mother rolled her eyes. "That's all well and good for you. I'm sure whomever you pick will have excellent financial prospects, a level head, and probably an interest in science."

"Exactly," he said.

"But that has nothing to do with what would interest *a girl!*"

He did not know how to respond to that. In his opinion, his sister wasn't the typical sort of girl at all. So, whatever would interest some generic girl would definitely not appeal to Gwen. But then again, he was a man, and therefore, unable to appropriately judge what Gwen or any other girl would want in a man. The preferences of the many women he'd met over the years had never made sense to him.

Which left him unable to satisfy his mother and thereby get her out of his bedroom. "Mother, what do you want me to do?"

"Get married to a girl who can help Gwen!"

"Seems a rather roundabout way of doing things."

She threw up her hands. "I give up. There is no talking to you."

Which is exactly what he had been thinking but would never say out loud. And then—in an absolute miracle—his mother spun on her heels and walked out. He stared after her, determined to memorize the conversation so he could repeat it whenever he wished to be alone. But in the meantime, he had his morning toilet to accomplish, plus he had remembered a few more tidbits from last night that he must get to his secretary before he forgot. It was the endless lifeblood of his political career, this memorizing of useful facts about people and families. Who had a talent for what and who was in need of it? If he could match the one with the other, then both owed him a favor, which he then applied to his political desires.

He would get his resolution passed no matter how many favors he had to curry because his conscience demanded it of him. And because his father had never fully recovered from his battle wounds—in mind or in body. In the end, Elliott believed that is what had killed him. Not the pneumonia, but the weakness that came from frequent nightmares and a pain in the hip and back that never eased.

If his father, despite all his advantages, had died from his military service, then what was to become of all the other soldiers? Those not well fed and with more grievous wounds? They were dying, or they were turning to thievery and worse to survive. It was a national disgrace, and so he would end it if he could. And in order to do that, he needed to return a blasted brooch to get a vote. Which meant he had best dress to meet Miss Gold right away.

He arrived barely on time and in his high perch phaeton. If anyone saw him—and he was sure they would—he planned to create a bit of mystery around who was the unknown woman sitting so openly in his carriage. His political influence traded on secrets, and it never hurt to dangle a bit of drama in front of gossipmongers just to see what other information he could glean in return.

He hopped down from his seat and entered the Dragon's Hoard jewelry store. It was a modest place but kept sparkling clean. The windows were nearly transparent as the sun streamed through to illuminate display cases of stunning jewelry fashioned in traditional and fantastic designs. And in the middle of the room sat Mrs. Dove-Lyon in her widow's weeds as she sipped her ever-present cup of tea. Standing nearby was Miss Gold's father, who looked refined and severe. Elliott had the brief impression that he was reporting to the headmaster's office for a hard dressing down.

Elliott turned on the charm beginning with the lady. "Good afternoon, Mrs. Dove-Lyons. I must say you are looking quite fine in this light. Your skin is like porcelain." What he could see of it, which was very little. The lady's face was veiled beneath a fine black netting, and only her mouth and chin were touched by the sun's rays. Then he turned to Mr. Gold. "An excellent day to you, sir. I have recommended your shop to a few of my intimates." Absolute truth. "I told them to drop my name and that you would assist them in finding exactly the kind of baubles they need. Though two of them had already heard of you. Your reputation is growing, Mr. Gold."

Meanwhile, he sniffed the air. "Is that a special blend of tea, Mrs. Dove-Lyon? I believe I scented it yesterday, and it has haunted my thoughts ever since." A bald-faced lie, but a harmless one. His thoughts, when they had wandered, went directly to the mysterious Miss Thisbe Gold and what she looked like beneath her plain scarf. Speaking of which, he looked around in confusion. "I don't see Miss Gold anywhere. I do hope she's not taken ill."

"Not ill," Mrs. Dove-Lyon said firmly. "Just waiting for the right moment to appear."

"Of course," he said. Mrs. Dove-Lyon did have a sense of the dramatic. "That's every woman's right, isn't it? To make us men burn with anticipation."

Mrs. Dove-Lyon didn't respond as he expected. In fact, she pursed her lips and said not a word. But her message was clear as one by one, very large men stepped out from the back of the room. He recognized them as the bouncers used in the Lyon's Den. Military men by the looks of them, all of them injured in some fashion but no less threatening.

And once a half dozen men had crowded into the back of the shop, Mr. Gold spoke. "My daughter is my greatest treasure," he said quietly. "And we all protect her."

"Of course—" he started to say, but Mrs. Dove-Lyon interrupted.

"I support your cause, Lord Byrn. Our veterans have been treated shabbily, and we wish the government took better care of them." She paused to see if he would interrupt, but he'd learned from the cradle that one did not interrupt a woman when she was delivering a *message*. It took a bit, but eventually, she continued to speak. "However, even broken, hurt, and ignored by the Crown, we take care of our own, and Miss Gold is definitely one of our greatest gems. I would hate to find out that your passions overran your good sense."

In other words, don't take advantage of Miss Gold. "I am counted a man of great sense, Mrs. Dove-Lyon." That was the absolute truth. Then he looked at Mr. Gold. "Your daughter is safe in my care. I stake my life on it."

"Yes, my lord," Mr. Gold said. "You do." And every man there nodded in agreement.

Well, that was chilling, and not the reception he was used to getting from the lower crust. But he was a man capable of listening, so he nodded. Such a show of brute support was rare for any woman—titled or not—and he was anxious to get to know the subject of such devotion.

Then—almost like magic—Miss Gold appeared. She stepped out from a hidden alcove behind the smallest display case. And when the light hit her face, he couldn't contain his gasp of surprise.

She was not beautiful; neither was she maimed in some way. Stupidly, he'd thought that she wore a scarf in the den to hide either exceptional beauty or a deformity of some kind. His best guess was an ethereal beauty given the amount of devotion of the men around her and the smooth, delicate way she moved. But there was none of that. Her face was average, her expression bland, and her clothing modest. And yet he couldn't stop looking at her.

She was *arresting,* and he couldn't figure out why. At least not until she stepped out from behind the counter, extended her hand to him, and smiled as if she were the Queen of England. "Good afternoon, Lord Byrn. Such a pleasure to see you again."

Poise. That was the word for it. Poise that stemmed from the confidence of knowing who you are and where you fit in the world. Never had he seen such assurance in a commoner, much less one so young and female. It drew his breath straight back into his heart, which squeezed tight. He found himself bowing over her hand and pressing her palm as a way of maintaining her touch. It was inappropriate given the number of hostile men staring at him. He released her hand reluctantly before mentally putting himself in order. He needed to be respectful, damn it, not gape at her like a boy at his first ball.

"The pleasure is all mine," he said, his tongue thick and unmanageable. "You look divine."

"I look respectable, unimportant, and uninteresting," she returned, "but that is the point, is it not? I'm a cousin from the Continent come to see a Joseph Wright portrait."

"Er, yes, but I meant what I said. You look divine." Because she did. Only a goddess could catch his attention so completely. He held out his arm, and she reached for it only to stop short. Stupid of him to have his forearm tense in reaction to her absence. She hadn't even touched him once, and yet he tightened in anticipation and grew impatient the longer she delayed.

"My sketchbook," she said, and one of the men handed over a well-worn book. She took it with a smile and a sweet, "Thank you." The man—six foot and with a missing ear—blushed down to the roots of his hair.

"Be safe, Miss."

"I'm sure I will be," she said with a warm smile, then she turned her face to the outside. Finally, she touched her fingers to Elliott's forearm, and he escorted her to the phaeton as if she were the queen. He certainly felt like his back was being peppered with angry glares from a legion of soldiers.

He helped her onto the bench, then took the reins. His boy servant, called a tiger, leaped into the vehicle from where he'd been holding the horses' heads, and they started off at a smart pace. Elliott wanted to get away from her corner of London and more into his own. He believed that would quiet his unusual reaction to Miss Gold.

It worked, a little. As soon as he had the horses under his command and the scenery moving past at a smart rate, his body relaxed, and he began to enjoy the afternoon. Which led him to the one thing he always did when happiness warmed his belly—he started asking questions.

"I'm afraid I don't know much about your family. Have you always lived in London?"

"We came when I was very young, just the four of us."

He counted the people he'd met. Father, grandfather, and her. "Your mother as well?"

"Yes. She died a few years ago."

"I'm so sorry. Do you remember your home country at all? Does your family miss it?"

She had been looking out at the passing street, but now turned to stare at him. "No and yes. Grandfather speaks of it every day. Why all the questions?"

He arched a brow. "I am curious about you. Are you offended?"

"No," she said slowly. "I just don't understand why. Given my father's display..." She rolled her eyes at that. "I doubt you intend seduction. I am a means to an end for you, a way to replace a brooch and thereby get a vote. So why the conversation? It is a beautiful day. I am happy to look at an area of London I so rarely get to see."

"You think I am only interested in seduction or a vote?"

Her brows rose as if that were obvious. "I am not of your class. What else could there be?"

"Friendship? Conversation?"

"With me?" She might as well have said, "With a zebra?"

He chuckled. "Of course, with you. In truth, I find every person fascinating from the lowest bootblack to the highest-born gentlemen in the land. But you are especially interesting."

"Why?"

Because she spoke with dignity and very little accent. Because there was absolutely nothing outstanding about her face or body, and yet he couldn't stop sneaking peeks at her. Because a half dozen rough men treated her like spun glass and blushed when she touched them. "Because you are the one who is here. I have already peppered Tom with questions." He jerked his head back at his tiger, who stood at attention behind them. "Go ahead, Tom. Tell her."

"He's right chatty, miss. Talks to everyone. T'aint cruel or stupid."

"Isn't cruel," Elliott corrected and was pleased to see Tom repeat the proper words in a clear tone.

"Isn't cruel. And he don't mind helping us better ourselves." There was enough emphasis on the letter *H* that Elliott didn't correct the rest.

Miss Gold frowned, but eventually, she nodded. "You have a kindred spirit in Mrs. Dove-Lyon. She has found ways to help all her employees improve their lot."

By trapping unwary men into marriage. He had heard of a few men who had taken missteps in her den only to find themselves caught in a bind they could not escape. And at least one of those unions had ended disastrously. "You sound as if you admire her."

"I do. She educates her girls. That alone is worthy of respect."

"You have the reforming spirit, then."

She smiled. "I am a smart woman. Of course, I wish to reform the world. I want as many opportunities as you."

"As a man? Or as a peer?"

She shook her head. "As a man, my lord. I know the world is not so open as to allow me to sponsor a resolution or bow before the king.

But if I had the opportunities of a man, then I should be content."

"Because you could openly create jewelry instead of pretend that it is your grandfather's work?"

She hesitated a moment, then shrugged. "Yes. And I could run the store as well or take a walk without fearing attack."

"Men fear attack as well."

"Not in the same way," she said.

That was certainly true. "Do you see no advantages to being a woman over a man?"

"You mean like carrying a child? Being at the creature's beck and call. To feed it, clothe it, teach it, all while the father is off—"

"Working hard labor to provide for you and the children."

"And drinking it away with his mates?"

That was a dark view of marriage, but he couldn't deny that it applied to so many. "Not all men drink what they earn."

She shrugged. "I suppose you are right. But I would rather do the work and leave someone else to carry the child."

"Hard labor hauling wares? Tilling fields?"

"Fashioning jewelry, my lord. That is my gift, if you recall. I merely wish to do it openly."

He could not fault her for that. "I shall make you a bargain. If you do a good job on the brooch, I shall commission something from you and tell everyone that you are the one who fashioned it."

Her eyes widened, and her mouth slipped ajar in shock. "Truly?"

"Yes. Of course."

She didn't take him at his word. Instead, she glanced back at Tom, who nodded.

"'E'll do it. 'E's a strange one."

Not exactly the ringing endorsement he expected. He shot his tiger a glare. "*He,*" he said.

Tom nodded. "*He's* a strange one."

Also, not the sentence he wanted repeated. He slanted a look at

Miss Gold. "Do we have a bargain?"

She shrugged. "It's not much of a bargain. I was going to do an excellent job anyway, but you are the judge and jury. There is nothing stopping you from saying the work is not up to snuff, and then away you go."

"You do not trust easily, do you, Miss Gold?"

"Why would I have reason to? My father and grandfather are honest, but the only other men I meet are the ones who wish to pawn their trinkets for money."

What a sad statement. "Those are not the best examples of mankind."

"No, my lord, they are quite often the worst."

"Well, I am counted one of the best. So, I shall endeavor to expand your experience of men." That was not phrased the way he intended, but she took it calmly enough. She even ventured a smile.

"I shall endeavor to see you in a better light and allow you to impress me."

And with that, he had to be content. Unfortunately, five minutes later, he proved exactly how inept he was.

CHAPTER THREE

THEY CONTINUED TO talk, getting to know each other in the most generic terms. He preferred spring with the promise of the coming year. She enjoyed the colors of fall and the crisp bite. Amber spoke easily with him, knowing that this day was a respite from the usual grays of her life. And as they talked, her artist eye caught the curve of a bird's throat as it broke into song. She saw a dewdrop catch the light on a spring bud. And she saw that everything smelled sweeter and looked cleaner as they progressed through London.

"Where are we going?" she asked. But even before the words were finished, he pulled the phaeton to the side, and his tiger sprang into action. The boy held the horses' heads while Lord Byrn set the brake, then leaped to the ground.

She smiled as he landed, appreciating the solid sound. Not light like a boy, not precarious as a drunkard, but firm and easy as a man in his prime. And truly, she could not help but notice the muscles of his thighs and the curve of his calves. She had no quarrels with Lord Byrn's form, that was for certain.

He handed her down, grabbed her sketchbook and pencil for her, then held out his arm to escort her to an impressive home such as she had never been inside. There was nothing distinctive about it except that it was clean, large, and in Mayfair. Amber found an unaccustomed spring in her step as they walked up the steps.

Lord Byrn knocked, and when a butler with a very large nose opened the door, he handed over his card. "Lord Byrn and Miss Thisbe—"

"Miss Amber Gohar," she corrected. She had no idea what prompted her to give her true name, correct surname and all, but the idea that she would step into a place so grand as anyone but herself was an insult to her pride. So she used her true name, and when the butler raised his eyebrows at her interruption, she shrugged. "He never pronounces it correctly."

"Quite right," Lord Byrn said. "I can be most muddleheaded about names." Then he patted her hand as if he were a fond uncle. "We've come to see the Joseph Wright portrait. Miss Gohar has a fondness for art, and we beg the countess's indulgence."

"Very well," the man intoned as he sketched a short bow. "Follow me, please."

They did while Amber eyed everything from the soaring column staircase to the dull wallpaper. They were escorted into a front parlor and asked about tea. Lord Byrn declined, but said, "No need to bother the countess. I'm sure she has better things to do than rattle around with us. We'll only be a moment."

The statement fell on deaf ears. The butler bowed himself out, leaving the door ajar such that a footman stationed in the hallway could eye them suspiciously. Lord Byrn fidgeted with his watch as they sat, his expression forced.

"What?" she whispered to him.

"I had hoped to catch the countess out. We'd have no problem otherwise. But if she is in the house…" His voice trailed away, and he looked chagrined.

"Is the woman difficult to charm?" Amber had already figured out that Lord Byrn's charisma smoothed his way as much as his title.

"The worst," he said with a funny groan. "She has heard too many pretty words in her life to enjoy any of them."

"Oh, dear. What will you do?"

"Use not-so-pretty ones." Then he shrugged. "But she's mostly immune to those, too."

And that was all they were able to say before an elderly woman dressed in the finest silks stepped into the room. She was announced not by the butler, but by a firm stomp of her cane and a piercing look.

"What is this about you and my portrait?" she demanded the moment she crossed the threshold. "You haven't shown the least interest before now."

Lord Byrn was on his feet, bowing over the countess's hand and giving her a very charming smile. "What very fine looks you are in today. Have you changed your hair? I do believe it is more fetching than ever."

"Yes, yes," she said with impatience. "Whyever do you want to see my portrait?"

"It's not for me, but for Miss Gohar, here. She has a particular fondness for the man's work, and I have promised her a visit to see it. It won't take but a moment—"

"Humph." She looked sternly at Amber, who curtsied as gracefully as she could. She'd never had to do so before such an intimidating lady, but Mrs. Dove-Lyon had taught it to them all. It was part of the regular deportment class that all the girls were expected to attend.

"I am most pleased to make your acquaintance, my lady," she said.

"We're not acquainted yet, now are we?" The dowager clomped over to her seat and settled in with Lord Byrn's help. Then she gestured to Amber. "Sit down, gel. Tell me about yourself."

Oh, dear. She had not planned a story with Lord Byrn. They'd talked of the weather, not of whatever he wished to say to the countess. Fortunately, she had spent much of her life daydreaming about who she would be back in Germany. Except the moment she opened her mouth, Lord Byrn rushed in to speak for her.

"Miss Gohar's mother and mine are distant relations, and when we learned that she would be traveling to London, Mama insisted that they visit. And then I was naturally all too eager to help. So here we are, hoping that you will indulge us. I've planned a visit to the Royal Academy as well." He ended with his charming smile again, though Amber could detect the strain in his features. It grew quite obvious as the countess stared at him. Eventually, he realized that she wasn't speaking, and he ventured a question. "Countess? Will you indulge us?"

"I already am," the woman retorted soundly. Then she turned to Amber and arched a brow. "I am waiting."

"My lady, there isn't much to tell," she began. And again, Lord Byrn opened his mouth to interrupt. He wasn't being rude, Amber realized. He really thought he was rescuing her.

"Countess, Miss Gohar is not used to—"

His words were cut off when she stomped her cane straight down upon his foot. To his credit, he didn't cry out, but he did wince. And while he was recovering, the countess spoke.

"I do hate it when a man thinks a woman can't speak for herself."

Amber had to struggle not to laugh. As it was, she was sure her expression reflected her merriment, and that made the dowager smile.

"Pray, continue," the woman ordered.

"I grew up in Berlin," she said, steadily warming to her fantasy. "My family has a moldering old castle in the country, but we rarely go. My great, great grandfather was a younger son, you understand, so the land is not ours and the connection distant. But I did love seeing all the art hanging there when I was a child on holiday."

"So, you live in the city?" the countess asked.

"We do. Papa is politically oriented, serving as secretary to..." She blew out a breath. "Well, it has changed recently as politics are wont to do. Mama helps him and, of course, looks after myself and my two younger sisters."

"No sons?"

"Alas, no. We are girls sent to find husbands."

"And so you are here? Visiting your mother's old friend and hoping to join the society whirl?"

Of course. That had been the fantasy where she ended up dancing with the prince who was not the Prince Regent but someone much more impressive. "Lord Byrn and his family have been so kind." But since she was not likely to enter the social whirl, she had to give an excuse as to why she would not be showing up at any balls. She leaned forward in a conspiratorial gesture. "May I tell you a secret, my lady?"

"A secret? Well, doesn't that sound dramatic?"

It did, and the countess loved it. "I am not so good at large parties. We were not in society in Berlin, and I am..." She gave an embarrassed shrug. "I am shy among so many august personages." She looked down at her sketchbook. "I am much more interested in London's art."

"My first ball was intimidating as well," the countess said. "I was trained as a young girl how to dance and play the harp, but nothing prepared me for the sheer magnificence of it all. So many people all looking at me."

Amber looked up, able to see it all in her mind. "I'll wager you were the magnificent one."

The countess harrumphed, but she was well pleased. "Of course, I was. My father made sure of it by commissioning the painting just before my presentation at court. Everything was done so that I was launched correctly. I caught the earl's eyes that very evening."

Amber smiled. "Did he dance with you?"

"Twice," she said with a fond smile. "I would have danced a third time, but twice was scandalous enough. My mother would have none of it."

"Oh, tell me everything," Amber begged. She wanted to know everything from the earliest dance lesson, through the color of the gown, all the way to what music was played, and how each and every gentleman appeared. It was like a fantasy come to life, hearing it from the woman who had done it all. And though part of her had outgrown fairy tales, this was like looking at a childhood dream with entirely new eyes, from a lady who had lived it.

So after gentle pleading, the countess relayed her memories in gorgeous fashion. Tea was served and drank, but Amber barely cared. So beautiful was the recitation and so different from anything she had ever experienced in her life. All her daydreams had been of showing up in a lovely gown and dancing. Suddenly, she had details that had never occurred to her before. Hair and gown designs, ways to maneuver her fan, and even how to flirt while still appearing modest. These were things she'd never considered before, and the dowager countess dropped them freely in every sentence.

Until the lady was done. She was tired, it seemed, though her eyes were misty with memories. "Oh my, how you have gotten me talking."

"I have loved every second," Amber said with complete honesty.

"Well then, come, come. Give it to me," the countess said as she waved her hand at Amber's sketchbook.

What? Oh no! The sketchbook did not show anything of Berlin or Germany. In truth, it didn't have much at all in the way of portraiture. It was jewelry designs and a few dreams. "No, my lady. Please. I am nothing but a dabbler."

For the second time that hour, the cane came down with force. Fortunately, Lord Byrn had moved his foot, so he was unharmed. This time, the irritation was directed at Amber.

"Show me, girl. I do not expect you to be Joseph Wright."

Amber looked desperately at Lord Byrn, and he tried to help. "She is most private about her sketches, Countess."

"Piffle. Modesty has its place but not right now." Then she held out her hand, and Amber had no choice but to pass her book over.

"These are new sketches," she hedged. "Nothing of home." That was a lie, but a necessary one. She had to explain why all of her sketches were set in London. Then she had to sit there in excruciating silence as the countess paged one by one through her sketches, while Lord Byrn looked over her shoulder.

No one said a word, but their faces were much too expressive. Lord Byrn's eyebrows rose higher and higher with each page. The countess, however, pursed her lips and frowned as time went on. Amber knew that she had only modest talent with sketches, but she was damned good with jewelry. She had to be. She *made* the pieces there on the page. The cat cufflinks with diamond eyes and the tiara fashioned to look like ivy with tiny ruby berries. She wasn't very good with pearls. That was her father's specialty, but she designed the metal that supported the strands.

Fortunately, many of the sketches showed jewelry on a person. Her best ones were given to her father to show potential customers. The dowager paused a long moment on a sketch of a distinguished woman with a cane sporting a wolf's head with ruby eyes. Lord Byrn appeared especially interested in a fanciful watercolor sketch of a couple dancing in the middle of a ball. She wore a breathtaking gown of palest blue. Sapphires adorned her ears, wrist, and lay tantalizingly above her décolletage. He was no less stunning, dressed in the latest fashion with a waistcoat that matched her sapphires in color and a cravat pin that looked like a cat leaping onto a pearl.

Finally, the countess finished her perusal. She looked up and spoke with a dry tone. "Well, I can certainly see where your interest lies. Gemstones do hold a particular fascination for many women." Her finger tapped on an intricate bracelet design of two dogs with garnet collars. They looked like they were running around the woman's wrist, and Amber thought it one of her best designs. Too bad she was

31

supposed to be interested in portraiture.

"They're just silly sketches," Amber said.

"They're extraordinary," Lord Byrn said, and she heard true admiration in his tone.

"Very well," the countess intoned as she pushed to her feet.

Both Lord Byrn and Amber echoed her movement, but he was the one who spoke. "We can see the portrait now? That would be a delightful cap to the afternoon."

"Now?" the countess said, outrage in her tone. "Of course not. I can't spend my entire day dilly-dallying around with you. You may see the portrait with everyone else, at my granddaughter's come out ball." She turned a piercing look on Lord Byrn. "I shall send Miss Gohar's invitation to your home, I presume?"

Lord Byrn blinked. "Er, no, actually. She is staying with my sister, Lady Dunnamore. Diana needed the companionship more than my mother."

The countess appeared to think on that a moment, then nodded. "Quite right. Quite right, indeed." Then she smiled at Amber. "I look forward to seeing you dance at the ball. I think you will find it exhilarating, just as I did at your age."

Meanwhile, Amber had just realized the countess expected her to attend her ball. Which made absolute sense given that she'd claimed to be in London specifically to attend parties and catch a husband. Which was wonderful! Except, of course, there was no way she could possibly attend. For one, Lord Byrn would never allow it. Nobs didn't allow common laborers into their events. And though she wasn't exactly a farmhand, she certainly wasn't exalted enough to attend.

"My lady," she breathed. "You are too kind." Then she added a slight cough because she was thinking ahead. Lord Byrn would need a reason for her not to attend, and a cold was as good as any.

"Nonsense," the dowager said as she herded them to the front door. "Now, off you go. Pick out a pretty dress for tomorrow night."

Tomorrow night? Oh, if only she could! But she knew her place, and it wasn't at the a come out ball. "If I could look at the painting now," she pressed. "I would be able to focus more on the dancing tomorrow."

"Enough modesty!" the countess said as she slammed down her cane hard enough that the sound reverberated through the house. "I will see you tomorrow night!"

And that was the end of that. In fact, the butler already had the front door open, and a footman was holding out Lord Byrn's hat.

CHAPTER FOUR

ELLIOTT STEPPED INTO the afternoon sunshine with his mind whirling. The details involved in maintaining their one little lie had just become cumbersome. He'd have to contact his sister and get her cooperation. Then there was the dress and the transportation, not to mention dancing instruction, and—oh hell—he'd have to get his mother to support the lie as well. She did have an old school friend in Germany. That was lucky—

Then Miss Gold let out a prodigious sneeze. It was loud, and it doubled her over on the steps.

"All you all right?" He supported her elbow as she straightened up and flashed an embarrassed smile behind her at the butler who had frozen with the door half shut.

"I do apologize. I hope I'm not getting ill." She turned and—leaning heavily on Elliott—made her way down the steps.

He supported her because that was what a gentleman was supposed to do. And he should not appreciate the delight of having her breasts pressed against his side or the view he had of them beneath her demure gown. But he was a man, and so he did. And while he was distracted, she looked up at him and spoke under her breath.

"No need to worry, my lord. Tomorrow night, you can claim I am laid low by a fever."

He had no intention of doing that. He'd seen how eagerly she'd listened to the tale of the countess's first ball. He had seen her desires drawn on the pages of her sketchbook. Elliott had sisters. He knew how much they dreamed of dancing in the arms of a handsome man. Certainly, he could give Miss Gold that. Indeed, it would give him great pleasure to see her attend a ball. But he also knew that she had pride, and so he found another excuse to give her the gift.

"Who would sketch the jewelry from the portrait?"

"Surely you are capable of that," she said as he handed her up into the phaeton.

He chuckled. "I assure you, I am not."

"One of your sisters, then?"

"Not likely. Diana sings beautifully, but her handwriting is appalling. And Gwen..." He shook his head. "Gwen reads. She does not sketch."

Then he climbed up, tipped his hat to Lord and Lady Prout, who were watching them with clear interest, and snapped the reins as he headed toward his sister's home. "I apologize. I had meant to take you to the Royal Academy to look at the art there, but it seems we have more pressing matters now."

He felt her jolt beside him and was a little insulted by her shocked stare.

"Whyever would you take me to the academy?"

"Because I said I would. Did you not think I was a man of my word?"

"You said that to the countess, not me. And as a way to pressure her into letting me see the portrait."

"Even so, I meant to do it."

He watched her absorb that with a slow nod. "And now?"

He shrugged. "Now I must take you to meet my sister Diana. She

35

will make sure you are set for tomorrow's ball. Is there anything you can think of that needs doing beforehand? Dress and gloves and the like will be managed by Diana, but do you need dance instruction? How quickly do you think you can learn it? Your curtsey was lovely, by the way. No fear there."

She slowly closed her mouth as she straightened until he thought her spine would crack. "You were judging my every action in there. Every word, every move to see if I would reveal my lowborn status."

He frowned. "I was not!" Not then, at least, but now he was going to present her to society. There were certain standards to maintain. She would not appreciate becoming a laughingstock any more than he would. "But I mean to help you tomorrow, and it will do us no good if you aren't prepared. Tell me what you need."

She stared at him. "I am not going to the ball. You can tell the countess I have a fever."

He shook his head. "I cannot, and I will not. As a general rule, I do not lie. There is already so much for me to remember that recalling lies is too exhausting. Therefore, I should very much like you to go to the ball with me tomorrow." He smiled at her. "Will you do me that honor, Miss Gold?"

She blinked. Once. Twice. And then she frowned. "Gohar. My real name is Amber Gohar. We changed it to Gold when we settled in London."

He nodded. "Ah. Then I am especially happy to introduce you to society under your true name." He leaned forward. "We are agreed?"

"I—" She cut off her word as she frowned at him. But he did not look away. And so, obviously flustered, she stammered out her agreement. "I, um, I w-would be pleased to go."

"Excellent," he said as they began moving through the London streets. "Now tell me what else you need. Shall I engage a dance instructor?"

"Er, no. I know the dances. Mrs. Dove-Lyon has an instructor who comes to the ladies' side of the den to teach girls while their mothers gamble."

"That's one way to increase business," he said dryly.

"In truth," she said, "I can dance both the men's and the women's part."

He chuckled. "No need for that."

"But the dress—"

"My sister should be able to help. We are nearly there."

His sister's London home was in an exclusive neighborhood that wasn't quite the peak of respectability. He knew it was an annoyance to his elderly brother-in-law that they hadn't managed a better residence, but some things only an old title could buy, and the Dunnamore title was a bit too Irish for that. Nevertheless, the man had done adequately for his family, and there was no shame in that. Elliott pulled to a stop and let his tiger jump down to hold the horse's heads as he disembarked. Then there was that delightful moment when he could grip Miss Gohar's waist as he helped her down. Her middle was solid with muscle, thin enough to carry off the best fashions, and situated below the most glorious breasts.

It wasn't gentlemanly of him to notice, but some things should be appreciated.

"My lord! So happy you are here."

Elliott turned in surprise to view his sister's butler stepping out of the house and waving him inside.

"My lord, please do come in!"

That was odd. He'd never seen a butler act so strangely. To come outside like this and wave him inside like a hawker pulling in customers. It was unseemly and—

The butler dropped his voice to a low hiss. "Hurry!"

Oh hell. Something was very amiss. "Excuse me," he said to Miss Gohar as he ran up the walk. The butler looked relieved as he held open the door. Then he pitched his voice very loud such that it echoed through the front hallway.

"Welcome, welcome, Lord Byrn. Your sister is in the library. Should I announce you?" He asked the question as he was shaking his head and actively pushing Elliott toward the back room.

Oh hell. "No need," he said as he rushed ahead and hauled open the library door. He expected to see blood everywhere or a fistfight or something to warrant the butler's odd behavior. What he saw instead looked absolutely proper, and yet the feeling in the room was horribly wrong.

His sister was backed against the massive library desk, and her stepson—a man ten years older than she and with twice the weight—lounged against the bookcase four feet away. He looked casual, smug, and as much of an ass as ever. His sister, on the other hand, was pale, and her hand trembled where it touched her throat.

"Hello, Diana," he said as he crossed the room quickly. "So sorry to barge in like this." He pulled her into a gentle hug that allowed him to whisper into her ear. "Are you hurt?"

"I'm fine," she whispered back, but there was no strength in the words just as there seemed to be little in her body. Her touch was fleeting, and even the kiss she bestowed was given more to the air than his cheek.

Despite her warrior-like name, his sister had always appeared delicate with fine features and a bell-like voice. She had a fairy-like beauty, but now she appeared withered. And that grieved him to no end. Why hadn't he known to stop this wedding twelve years ago?

He turned to address the Dunnamore heir. "Geoffrey, how odd to see you dressed before tea." The man usually roused himself only to go to the dens and whorehouses.

"I've come to dance attendance on my father and dear step-mama." He didn't even attempt to hide the sneer in his voice, but far worse was the leer he gave Diana. "Father asked me quite specifically to escort her to a...party for some entertainment."

He paused before the word *party* was a clear threat. Everyone here knew his sort of entertainment would not match Diana's.

"Excellent," Elliott cried, much to everyone's surprise. "We shall all go together then, as I have come specifically to beg my sister's indulgence."

No fool, Diana nodded her head. "I will always come to your aid, Elliott. How can I help my favorite brother?"

It was a joke. He was her only brother, but it showed him that there was spirit left in her despite her years in this horrendous marriage. Slightly relieved, he crossed to the library door where the butler had just escorted Miss Gohar. He took her hand, oddly pleased that her skin was rough with callouses and had strength. His sister's frailty had never appealed to him.

"You recall mother speaking of her friend's daughter? This is Miss Amber Gohar from Berlin, newly come to town. Mother extended an invitation to stay with us, of course, but we are filled to the rafters without a chamber to spare." That wasn't remotely true, but it would serve as an excuse. "We had hoped that you have room to spare for her. The Dowager Countess of Morthan has expressly invited her to her granddaughter's ball tomorrow—"

"And you need help getting everything set, don't you?" his sister asked.

Miss Gohar curtsied very neatly and spoke in a quiet voice. "It's all very rushed," she said. "I have only just arrived in London and—"

"Already, you have an invitation to an exclusive event. How exciting."

But then Geoffrey had to insert himself into the conversation like the boor he was. "You came all the way from Berlin alone? Without a chaperone?"

Oh hell. What to say to that? But Miss Gohar had a ready answer. Her expression fell, and he believed her eyes actually watered. "I traveled with my grandmother, but the French air did not suit her."

Her expression took on a tragic look. "She is resting with relations in Calais, but she pressed me to continue on. She did not want me to miss my chance, you see."

"Of course not," Diana said. "That was very gallant of her and very brave of you to travel the rest of the way alone."

Clearly, Amber had a talent for the boards, but in this case, it was very helpful. Elliott flashed his sister a smile. "Could you help us, please?"

"You mean find a bedroom in this huge empty house?" She smiled sweetly at Miss Gohar. "It's just me and my husband, you see, with bedchambers everywhere." She looked up at her butler. "Simpson, could you see that a room is prepared?"

The butler bowed. "Right away, my lady."

"Why don't you go with him?" Elliott suggested. "Show Miss Gohar about while I take a moment to speak with Geoffrey."

His sister nodded, flashing him a grateful smile. She knew he intended to act as the brother he hadn't been when she was seventeen. He only hoped it would work.

Both men waited until the ladies departed. Geoffrey made his way to the brandy and poured himself a large measure. Elliott waited until the man filled his glass and turned around to lean heavily against the sideboard. His expression was flippant, and his smile oily. And that made Elliott's protective instincts burn.

"What were you arguing about with my sister?" Elliott asked as he adopted an equally casual pose.

Geoffrey waved his glass at a heavy candelabra on the desk. "She objected to my pinching the silver."

Elliott felt his jaw drop in shock. "You admit to being a thief?"

"I am nothing of the sort!" Geoffrey exploded. "It is *my silver!*" He drained the last of his glass. "My brandy, my furnishings, my home! If I require the silver, then I am within my rights to take it."

"No, Geoffrey, it's not," Elliott said firmly. "It is your father's until his death and after the will has been read, and not one moment before."

"Well, then," he said as he stepped forward. His face was ruddy with drink, which meant the brandy was not his first glass today. Worse, the menace in him was palpable. "I find myself in arrears with my landlord. If I cannot pay him, then I shall be forced to return to the family home to reside. I will move in here. Immediately."

With Diana? And her nearly bed-ridden husband? That was not acceptable. "This home is occupied. I suggest you return to the family seat in Yorkshire."

"That moldering old place? Haven't been there in ages and have no desire to return." His grin was especially hateful. "So, if you have no wish for me to be in close quarters with my dear step-mama, then perhaps you could see your way to helping me out?"

The blackguard was larger and older than his step-mama, and there was no telling what he would do if he lived here. The idea was insupportable. But neither could they give in to blackmail. Geoffrey was an endless well of need. If Elliott once gave in to paying his bills, then nothing would stop the demands or the threats.

"And that candelabra," Elliott said, gesturing to the heavy thing. "That will cover you?"

"Heavens, no. I had thought to hit my landlord over the head with it," he said as if it were a joke, but with Geoffrey, one could never tell.

Elliott was beginning to see the rationality in letting the man pinch the silver. If the other choice was to have him harassing his sister night and day, then why not let the man have his inheritance early? Except that every bone in his body objected to the very idea. He took that moral outrage and his complete loathing of the man and poured it into his next words.

"Very well," he said softly. "Take the candelabra now and, by all means, kill your landlord with it. I, for one, will relish seeing you hang for murder."

Geoffrey grinned and sauntered over to the silver. But Elliott wasn't done. He crossed the room quickly and set his hand around the heavy piece just before Geoffrey did. And he used his considerable strength to keep it on the desk.

"Take it now and never come here again."

"My father is dying," Geoffrey said. "I must be here."

He was probably thinking of bashing his father over the head. "I don't care. You will not see my sister, you will not speak to her, and you will not even breathe the same air as her."

"Or what?"

"Or I shall beat you with your own silver." He put on his own oily grin. "I know how to do it and *not* hang." That was a lie. He had no idea how, but he knew someone who did, and he would visit Lord Lucifer before the sun rose tomorrow. "Have I made myself clear?"

Geoffrey didn't look in the least bit intimidated. Instead, he drained his brandy glass. "If you think to frighten me, old boy, recall that I have more connections in the underworld than you. And if I choose to murder anyone, not a soul would know except me."

"I am not your father," Elliott said firmly. "I do not issue empty threats."

"Hmm," Geoffrey drawled. "And neither of you understand how far a desperate man will go to get what's his."

"It's not yours."

"Yet."

If ever a single word sounded like a threat, it was that one. By his own admission, Geoffrey was desperate, and that made him dangerous. Elliott revised his earlier estimate. He would speak with Lord Lucifer within the hour. Meanwhile, he released his hold on the candelabra.

"Take the silver and be gone. You are not welcome here."

Geoffrey grabbed the heavy piece and brandished it aloft. "Good heavens, you sound like that's supposed to be a revelation. I haven't

been welcomed in my father's house since I was in leading strings."
Then he moved casually to the door, picking up the ormolu clock on
the way. "Your sister, on the other hand," he said with a leer, "I find
her to be most welcome. Most welcome, indeed."

It was a lie because Geoffrey's entire family had objected to the
marriage. None of the children had welcomed her nor been remotely
kind, which was especially hard as she was younger than the lot of
them. But that was water under the bridge. Right now, Elliott had to
find a solution for his sister that didn't involve someone risking the
hangman's noose.

Fortunately, the staff appeared to be on his sister's side. The butler,
Simpson, had been incredibly anxious to have Elliott intercede. In fact,
the old guy stood sentry, and his jaw clenched as Geoffrey grabbed his
hat and departed.

Meanwhile, Elliott joined Simpson at the door. "Your staff seems
to be somewhat thin of sturdy, young footmen," he said. "It would be
a kindness, I think, for you to provide employment for our veterans.
They need good work to do."

Simpson winced. "If I might be candid, my lord?"

"Please."

"The estate is crumbling. His lordship's health has been declining,
so he has not seen to things as he ought. And so…" He sighed. "There
are no funds to pay such new servants."

That made sense. If the heir was a disaster, too often, the father
was as well. "You leave that to me." He wasn't exactly flush with
money, but for his sister's welfare, he would find a way to pay for her
protection. He only hoped it was enough. "Pray inform my sister and
Miss Gohar that I had an appointment and will return in two hours."

"Of course, my lord." Then he handed Elliott his hat and bowed
deeply before holding open the front door.

Elliott wasted no time in turning the horses' heads to the Lyon's
Den. He hadn't seen his quarry except as a glimpse of someone

slinking into the shadows last night, but it had been enough. He arrived at the Den during the midafternoon heat, which was more damp than hot. He pushed his way inside and searched until he found Titan plucking a guitar in a dark basement bedroom. His face was tight, and his scarred hand moved with difficulty across the strings. Odd that it was the man's ears that gave him away. His hair was shorn close, and there was a unique fold of ear that betrayed his identity.

"Luke, what the hell are you doing?" he said by way of greeting. "Your entire family thinks you're dead."

The desultory plucking at the instrument stopped. When the man spoke, his words were barely intelligible thanks to a thick accent of no particular origin. "You must be mistaken, milord. I ain't—"

"Stop it," Elliott ordered as he stepped inside the dank room and shut the door. "You are Luke, future Earl of Wolvesmead. Your brother and I enjoyed an entire summer crawling around your dilapidated castle with you." It had been perhaps the best months of his childhood. "Your mother spends hours on her knees every day, praying for your safe return. Does she know you're alive? Does anyone?"

Luke's eyes narrowed, but that was the only reaction. He remained as he was, shrouded in shadow with his maimed hand resting lightly on the guitar. "I don't know what ye mean—"

Elliott blew out a breath. "I'm not here to banter lies with you, Luke. I need your help. Diana is in trouble. You remember her, yes? She's of an age with you."

Luke's head lifted the rest of the way until his haunted eyes looked out from a gaunt face. "I remember her. Married Dunnamore."

At least he wasn't denying his identity anymore. "Her stepson Geoffrey is threatening her. I need a man in her house to protect her until I can think of a better solution. I've enough to pay you—if you want it—and another footman besides."

Luke's mouth twisted down. "I know the blighter. He's got a crew of fellows who act like a gang of bloody thieves."

"If they would stop at thievery, I would be less afraid."

Luke grimaced. "You can't count on that."

"I know. Which is why I need you to stop playing wolf pack here and—"

"Play wolf pack there?"

They were referring to what the widow Dove-Lyons called her bouncers. She'd named them her Wolf Pack with Titan (Luke) as their leader. Elliott couldn't think of a better group to look after his sister. "Do you have trustworthy men who could use the extra blunt?"

"They're all good men," Luke snapped.

Of course, they were. Luke wouldn't tolerate anything less. "Then you'll help me?"

The man took a while to answer. He stared into the shadows for a moment, and his entire body stilled until he became one with the darkness. But in the end, Luke dipped his chin in agreement. "I will help on one condition."

"Anything."

"You won't tell anyone who I am."

Which name was forbidden? Titan (his Lyon's Den name), Lord Lucifer (his boyhood nickname), or Luke (his real name)? It didn't matter. Elliott would not be party to deceiving a man's family. "Your brother is my friend. Your whole family is in hell wondering if you're—"

"They think I'm dead. They've accepted it."

"But you're not!" Elliott took a step forward. "And your mother definitely hasn't—"

"Believe me, she has. Or if she hasn't, she's praying that I stay away."

"That isn't true." But then Elliott remembered his summer at Wolvesmead Castle. Luke's mother had never been a warm woman. She had a critical eye, a sharp tongue, and an unrelenting anger toward her eldest son. Elliott never asked the reason for it, but he couldn't deny it. "Think of your brother, then, and your father."

Luke's head dropped, and he began picking at the guitar again. "Find someone else," he said over the plunking notes.

Elliott stood there a while, too aware that he had no other options. He still tried to find a different way. He pulled up an old stool and squatted down on it as he tried every manipulative technique he knew. He employed reason, wielded guilt, even took a stab at patriotism. None of it worked. In the end, he gave in to Luke's demands. Diana was worth the sacrifice, though he couldn't shake the feeling that he was betraying one of his oldest friends in order to save his sister.

"Very well," he conceded. "How quickly can you start?"

"Immediately," Luke said as he set aside the guitar. "But you can't have them call me Titan. You can't mix your sister with the Lyon's Den."

An excellent point.

Luke grabbed his hat. "Call me, Mr. Lucifer."

Elliott snorted. "Don't be ridiculous. Mr. Dunderhead would be more fitting."

Luke grabbed a pair of knives and slipped them into unseen pockets. "You never understood the intimidation of a good nickname."

Very true. Names meant nothing to him, and a nickname was less substantial than smoke. Still, he trusted Luke to know his business, and if that meant calling him Mr. Lucifer, then he would oblige. Besides, Elliott was anxious to get back to Amber and didn't want to waste the time to argue. "Take whatever alias you like so long as you're there tonight to protect Diana."

"From Geoffrey? My pleasure," Luke said. Then he smiled in a way that seemed truly satanic. "I shall keep her as safe as a vestal virgin."

Elliott opened the bedroom door with a snort. "You're mixing mythologies, you know. Greek, Christian—"

"Vestal virgins are Roman."

"Fine. Roman and Christian."

Luke adjusted his clothing, his body limber despite his ruined hand. "We can make plans as we take your chariot to Diana's temple."

"Good God, when did you become so fanciful?"

"I gave up reality when forty-eight thousand men died at Waterloo."

Elliott winced. "I thought the number was twenty-three thousand."

"Is it any less horrendous because the other twenty-five thousand were French?"

No, it wasn't. Every man had a mother, and every death marked a loss. In the end, Elliott had nothing to say but, "I'm sorry." He had not fought in the battle. He had not seen the blood, smelled the gore, or heard the screams. He was not haunted as Luke so obviously was. But he could still grieve the destruction even as he lay the blame fully upon the Corsican emperor. "Thank God it's over."

"Is it?" Luke challenged.

No, it wasn't, but that was why Elliott was working so hard to get his resolution passed. He needed to end the misery for so many, including the newest member of Diana's household—Mr. Lucifer.

CHAPTER FIVE

A MBER FOLLOWED THE butler and Lady Dunnamore up the stairs. She tried to look with a critical eye. It was the only way she could combat the overwhelming sense of giddiness at being inside a majestic old home, at walking behind a lady who moved like she floated upon the air, and at being an imposter to a woman who seemed beset by her own troubles.

She tried to be unimpressed but failed. Amber saw the peeling wallpaper but was left awed by the fine portraits hanging upon it. She noticed the thin fabric on the chairs but smelled the beeswax that glossed the wood to a shine. The staff was meticulous, she saw, but the family did not spend on upkeep. This wasn't a surprise as the blighter, Geoffrey, had been to the Lyon's Den often. He had pawned jewelry there, he had played deep and lost, and he had been escorted off the premises when he had become too drunk to hold a pair of dice.

"Lord Dunnamore rests in there," Lady Dunnamore said in the barest voice. "My chamber is there." She pointed to the room next door. "And you shall be here," she said as stepped into a bright yellow room set directly beside her bedroom. "It only needs an airing and bedding. That shan't take long. In the meantime, you must come into

INTO THE LYON'S DEN

my room, and we will look at what gowns can be fitted to you."

"None of them, I'm afraid," Amber said. Lady Dunnamore was thin and light. Amber, on the other hand, had a larger chest, rounder hips, and muscles that added bulk.

"Don't be too sure," the lady said as she eyed Amber. "I've thinned in the last few years. I'm sure I can find something that will serve."

"My lady, please. I don't wish to impose—" she began, but Lady Dunnamore cut her off.

"Why don't we talk in my bedchamber as yours is being set right? I am quite curious, you know. Mama said so little about you."

Her Mama had said nothing of her at all, but Amber had no way to know if she was impersonating a real person who was the daughter of Lady Byrn's friend or someone completely imaginary. Either way, she couldn't construct a story until she learned the facts from Lord Byrn. Unfortunately, his sister wasn't giving her any choice as she held open her bedroom door and gestured Amber inside.

"Come in," she said in a soft voice. "Only we must keep our voices down. Lord Dunnamore's rest is easily disturbed."

"Of course, Lady—"

"Hush." She carefully shut her bedroom door and then went to press her ear against the door that adjoined with her husband's room. They could both hear the snores that came from inside. So with a smile, the lady turned back to Amber. Except the smile was not friendly. It showed teeth and did not reach the ice in her blue eyes. "What is your real name?" she asked quietly.

"Amber Gohar, my lady."

"I will have the truth. All of it."

"I have no wish to burden you, my lady. It was not my idea to involve you."

The woman nodded, and though she seemed like a stiff wind could blow her aside, the look she settled on Amber had weight. A distinctly uncomfortable weight, and Amber barely restrained herself from shuffling her feet like a guilty child.

"Did you know that Elliott inherited his title when he was twelve years old?" she asked.

This question was asked in a casual manner at distinct odds with her heavy stare. Amber wasn't sure what to make of it, so she answered in the politest tones. "I did not know that, my lady."

"I was the eldest, so I had to keep things going. It was years before he was old enough to pay attention, you know. So it fell to me."

"Not your mother?" Amber's mother had died years before, but when alive, she had been a force to be reckoned with. She kept all the men in line and raised Amber with a stern hand.

Diana shook her head. "My mother did what she thought best."

That was not a compliment to her mother.

"Once my brother grew of age, he fought for me, my mother, and my sisters. Nothing was easy, and my husband was cruel to him. And yet, he found a way, and I am in a better place because of it."

That was a surprise. Just how bad had it been? And what had Lord Byrn done to make it better? Questions swirled in her mind, but she kept her mouth shut. It wasn't her place to ask.

"Suffice it to say that I am extremely grateful to my brother, and so I will do whatever he asks to the best of my ability. Whatever that means regarding you."

"That is extraordinarily kind of you."

"It is nothing of the sort," she answered, her tone growing more tart. "It is what I will do for my family." Then her voice took on more volume and strength. "Which means I will also destroy anyone who harms him, and in the most humiliating way possible. Do I make myself clear?"

The threat was clear, as was the steel inside Lady Dunnamore. It was impressive, and Amber responded with a meek, "Yes, my lady. Perfectly clear." Except that was not her only response.

This whole situation was like something out of her dreams. That she should attend a ball or even spend a night as a guest of a true lady was akin to her dream of dancing with the prince. None of it felt real, and tiny champagne bubbles of giddiness tickled her insides. They teased her sense of humor and made her smile when she should be curtseying like the lowest maid.

"Do you think I am jesting with you?" Lady Dunnamore demanded.

"No, my lady. Definitely not." Amber did her best to school her voice and expression to one of deepest contrition. But she couldn't. She was just too happy.

She was living out one of her favorite daydreams, where she was the poor relation of a lonely woman of means. Where she arrived at the house, brought friendship to the lady, and one day was able to attend a ball where she danced with a handsome man. Some days it was the prince. Other days, he was a king already. And sometimes, he was quite simply the fiercest and most handsome warrior in the land.

"Then why—"

"I did not ask to come here. That was his lordship's idea. But now that I am here, I find I like you quite well and will be pleased with whatever time I get to share with you." That was true, although not the whole truth since she was not going to talk about her dream of going to a ball.

Her ladyship frowned for a moment, then lifted her chin. "Will you tell me everything?"

Amber bit her lip. "Perhaps you should ask your brother."

"I am asking you."

And here, Amber had a choice. She could confess all, or she could invent another story from her fertile imagination. She could pretend all sorts of nonsense, and she had a large store of fantasies from which to draw. The need to spin a tale burned on her tongue, but Lady Dunnamore deserved better. Why? Because her stepson was the blighter Geoffrey, and so her life could very well be a disaster of his making.

"I am a tradeswoman," she finally said, feeling her cheeks heat in embarrassment. If Lady Dunnamore wished to humiliate her, this was the best way. "Your brother needs me to fashion a brooch for him made exactly as appears in Lady Morthan's portrait."

"And you cannot see it except at the ball?"

Amber shook her head. "We tried, but she refused."

"And issued an invitation instead?"

"Insisted, my lady."

Lady Dunnamore blew out a breath. "My brother cannot afford to dismiss her. Her family is quite political."

"So, I have come to understand."

Amber waited a long moment as the woman seemed to inspect her from head to toe. She frowned as she did so, as if she were looking at a dirty child. "It won't serve, Miss Gohar."

"What?" Amber bristled. She would have said a great deal more, but the lady held up her hand.

"You cannot be the daughter of one of mother's lost friends. Mother doesn't have any lost friends. Enemies, perhaps, but she will never admit that she sponsored one of their children. You must be the younger sister of one of mine." She frowned. "From Berlin, you say?"

She hadn't said, but her brother had. "Yes, my lady."

"And we can't have any of that either. You will call me Diana, and you shall be Amber."

The very idea that Lady Dunnamore would call her by her given name made her eyes water with gratitude. She was Thisbe to the aristocracy who frequented the Lyon's Den. *Daughter* to her father and *child* to her grandfather. None but her dead mother had ever called her by her given name. Until now. Until Lady Dunnamore opened up her home and her closet to her. Even knowing that it was done for her brother did not dim the warmth in Amber's heart. They were to be friends, and the enormity of that made every part of her flush with gratitude.

"You are too kind," she managed.

"And you had best not be lying."

"I am not," she said firmly.

Diana smiled, then threw open her wardrobe. "Then let us see what can be done for tomorrow night."

The answer was clear. A very great deal could be done. Lady Dunnamore had plenty of gowns and a maid who was a wizard with needle and thread. They barely noticed when her brother sent a message up that he had an errand and would return in a couple hours. Amber was measured as they discussed colors. They enjoyed a late tea while analyzing trends in fashion. In this, Amber had a great deal of knowledge thanks to the women who frequented the ladies' half of the Lyon's Den. And then they laughed together as Amber encouraged Diana to reminisce.

The woman was indeed lonely, and she needed little prodding to speak fondly of her childhood and especially her brother's antics. He had been a lively boy and a late addition to a mother who had produced only girls. They feared, at first, that he would grow up to be timid beneath so many women. Quite the contrary, Elliott had joined forces with the gardener's sons and the village boys. They became the terror of the county, and if it were not for the stern hand of Diana's father, he might very well have run roughshod over everyone.

"My father knew just how to encourage a little boyhood wildness without letting it get out of hand. And he instilled in Elliott what it means to be a responsible head of the family." At this, Diana's eyes grew misty. "His death was a great blow."

To everyone, it seemed, because Elliott had spoken briefly about his own grief when his father passed. "My father never recovered from my mother's death. I miss her terribly."

A bond was established between her and Diana, one forged in fabrics, fashion, and similar loss. It seemed Diana relished having someone to talk with as much as Amber treasured a friendship with a lonely woman with a fiercely loyal heart. That was something Amber understood. Which made the afternoon fly by until Lord Byrn had the audacity to return.

It was late, and the Lyon's Den had opened an hour before. Amber was needed in the cage with her grandfather, and this daydream-come-to-life was ended. She had to go back to work. They were downstairs in the front parlor laughing over the antics of Lady Dunnamore's tiny dog, but the moment she heard Lord Byrn's voice in the hallway, Amber began her apologies.

"I am so grateful, my lady," she said, regretting the need to use the honorific instead of "Diana."

"Stop, stop! You cannot mean to leave. We were having such a lovely time."

Amber didn't answer. The ache in her heart was enough to clog her throat. Stupid, stupid to grow attached to a daydream. She had plenty of friends at the Lyon's Den. The women who worked the upstairs rooms and the dealers all treated her as a treasured sister. She didn't need another friend, she told herself. And yet, her time with Diana had made her wish for something more. Something that had colors like the fabric on Diana's settee. Something that did not smell of tobacco or spirits. As if she, too, were the willowy lady of an old title who might one day dance with a prince.

Except it was a dream, and so when Lord Byrn entered the parlor, she stood and made her goodbyes. He had no time beyond a quick buss on his sister's cheek before they both were outside and headed back to the gray cage in which Amber spent the bulk of her time.

Quick day, quick end.

For the first time in her life, she hated her life with a passion born of despair. Because she knew with absolute certainty that she would grow old and die in the gray cage at the Lyon's Den.

CHAPTER SIX

E LLIOTT LIFTED AMBER into the phaeton and took too long to do it. Already, he had been hither and yon in London, and he had a full evening ahead. Was it so wrong for him to linger over the smell of a woman? To feel, however briefly, the fullness of her hips, the swell of her breasts, and the strength in her legs? She gripped his shoulders, and he saw her lips part as her body brushed against his. She was light enough that he did not need to hold her so close. But he did so because her body was luscious, and he had been too long without a woman.

Plus, she had the most spectacular eyes. They were hazel, turning blue or green according to her mood. Right now, they were shifting to blue as she locked gazes with him. And her lips were wet and open, parted in surprise or interest or sheer temptation. He didn't know, but his imagination certainly supplied details that were best left unspoken.

And yet, he did think and linger until it became unseemly. So, he stepped back. It's what a gentleman should do. But in his thoughts, they were doing something else entirely.

He jumped into the phaeton, using the time to rein in his runaway feelings. And once the horses were moving at a smart clip, he kept his eyes on them, but his words were for her.

"How much time will you need to gather your things for tonight?"

She jolted beside him. "What?"

"Your things for tonight. Tomorrow as well, I think. Balls end very late, and you will want to rest afterward."

"But…" She took a quick breath. "Who will work in the cage tonight?"

Now it was his turn to jerk in surprise. "In a *cage*?" The very idea was appalling.

"Yes. All the valuables are kept behind bars. My grandfather and I are there as well as…" She almost said Lina, but quickly switched to the Den name. "The Abacas Woman." Lina had a character name from *A Midsummer Night's Dream*, but no one ever remembered it. She was simply the woman who click-clacked her abacas as she counted out money. Her exotic voice added to the mystery since she never showed her face.

"I suppose it's safer," he finally said, though the idea of her locked every night behind bars horrified him. "But surely, you did not think to work tonight."

She stiffened. "I surely did. Why wouldn't I?"

"Because you are to stay with my sister. I thought you liked her. I thought you'd want to."

"I do!" Her hands twisted in her lap. "I definitely do, but…" She exhaled slowly. "This is all so sudden. I don't know what my grandfather will do without me."

He looked at her. "You can't be absent for one night? Your grandfather must have done the work alone at some point."

"Two nights," she corrected primly. "And… of course, he can. My father helped when I was younger or sick."

"Then there is nothing to prevent you from taking a couple nights with my sister, yes?"

"Yes," she said slowly, a low tension in her voice. And when she didn't continue, he pressed her.

"Why do you sound so glum?"

"I...I don't know," she answered with a frustrated harrumph. "I am being illogical. I was just thinking how much I wished to stay with Diana, and now that I might, I am angry with you."

"With me?" he said, the words startled out of him. "Whatever have I done?" Except get her an invitation to a ball and set her up for a lovely holiday with his sister.

She turned to face him on the bench. "You have completely upset my days."

He snorted. "You are a creature of habit, then."

"Absolutely not! I despise habit, routine, and the hideous sameness of my days."

There was such vehemence in her tone that she confused him even more. "Then why are you angry at me?"

She folded her arms and twisted back to stare out over the horses' heads. Her words came out low and grumpy. "I told you I was being illogical."

Yes, she had. And wasn't that a surprise? Not that a woman could be irrational. His mother, for example, seemed to take pride in twisting things around until black became white and up became down. But Amber was not only aware of her strange thoughts but admitted to them. That was a rarity, even among elite men. And so, he found himself admiring her, even as he poked at her.

"Can you not try to use a little reason?" He kept his tone light because he was teasing her. And thankfully, she did not take offense.

"I am angry," she finally said, "because, after two lovely days, I shall be returned to my cage, and everything will feel so much worse."

"You will have some delightful memories, I hope."

"I will," she said wistfully. "I only wish..."

"That your life could always be parties and fashion discussions over tea?"

"Yes," she said, the glumness returning to her voice.

For a few moments, he thought on the difficulties of her life. Every night she sat in a cage and assessed jewelry sold to her family by dissolute men of the worst sort. By day, she fashioned jewelry, likely in another back room. She had little company, few diversions, if any, and probably saw the best years of her life slipping away.

"Is there some way that you have fun? Perhaps a young man who brings you posies and sweetmeats?" The idea didn't sit well with him, but that was his lust speaking. She was a desirable woman, so naturally, he wanted her for himself. "Perhaps one of those large men who were threatening me earlier today."

"There is a man," she said softly. "A prince who dances divinely. He brings me flowers and writes poetry. He dresses in bright colors and laughs like a violin played very fast." She turned to him, and she seemed to be looking at his face as she spoke, comparing him feature to feature with this prince. "His nose is strong and his jaw hard, and his eyes sparkle like emeralds in the sun." Her gaze traveled away from him now to the sky as the sun set with brilliant colors. "He'll be a great leader someday, but for now, he spends his time studying the great thinkers of the world." She shot him a wry look. "And writing me poetry, of course. Truthfully, he's not that good at it, but I love every word."

"And does he sing arias to you as well?" There was a sourness in his tone that he didn't like, but he couldn't stop.

"Oh, naturally," she said. "And at that, he's *very* good."

He didn't respond at first. Simply sat there and guided the horses while, inside, he was envisioning her stretched out on a bed while this paragon read poetry to her. Later, he would set the book aside and stroke her body with a leisurely caress. The bastard had clear intent, but she was too innocent to know and too enraptured by his words to notice when his hand traveled to indecent places.

"Who is this prince?" he demanded gruffly. "Where is his kingdom? Have I met him?" He expected that she would say the nearby bakery or tinker stall, maybe a haberdashery. Didn't they all style themselves as kings of their respective trades? He did not expect her sudden peal of laughter.

"He's not real, you goose! I made him up years ago when I started working every night in the cage. It can get boring in there, and so when I tire of sketching, I look out at the men on the floor and imagine them better. Smarter, sweeter, and more interested in me than in the dice or cards." She snorted. "That last part is the most important."

It would have to be. And didn't he feel stupid for feeling jealous of an imaginary man? "A prince, you say. Why not a king?"

"Because they are busy ruling their kingdom. A prince has time to play."

"Of course." He relaxed into the game now that he knew none of it was real. "And is this a prince of England? Or of some other clime?"

"Most times, it's here. I have spent nearly all my life in London, and so why not become Queen of England? Other times he is from a very warm, sunny place with bright flowers and fruits that can be plucked from trees that grow everywhere."

"You are imagining Spain or Italy, then. Africa is too hot and the colonies too far away."

"Oh no," she said. "I have read of islands in the middle of the ocean with turtles and huge birds."

He nodded. "The Galapagos, then." The British navy had discovered it some thirty years ago. "James Colnett was a friend of my father. He is the one who drew the navigation charts. Every night, I would pester him until he told me about the giant turtles or the birds with blue feet."

"Birds with blue feet? Truly?"

"Like a seagull only much smaller. White neck and face, black wings, and bright blue, webbed feet."

She sighed. "How I wish I could see that." Then she smiled. "It's decided. My prince is definitely from Galapagos. After we're wed, I shall lay every day in the sunshine and watch the blue-footed birds. And then at night, I will go into the shop and fashion their likeness in silver and gold. Sapphires for their feet, diamonds for their eyes, and black onyx for the wings."

He turned to her, surprised. "You shall work even when you're a queen?"

"Fashioning jewelry is not work, my lord. It is the happiest part of my day." She glanced at him. "Save talking fashion over tea and attending a ball."

"Save that, of course." It was a good thing that she took joy in her family's trade. So many did their work merely because their fathers and grandfathers had. They went through the motions as their attention wandered to something else entirely. But even though she apparently loved it, he still thought her life restricted. "Surely, there is a real man who has caught your attention. You are an attractive woman. I wager many men are looking at you. Do you not look back at any of them?"

Were he to ask such a thing of a woman in his own set, he would be handed a severe dressing down, and rightly so. It was an impolite question. But she was a tradeswoman and he a lord. Some questions were allowed, provided the lady herself was not insulted.

"They have looked, to be sure," she said, her voice muted. "They look at the gemstones in the shop and at the fine wool I wear for all that it is a dull brown."

"You have been hurt by some blighters, then. I am sorry for it."

She snorted. "All women of means have been hurt by blighters. I begin to think there are no honest men left."

"You cannot judge all men by those who frequent the Lyon's Den."

She nodded. "Of course not. But you live among the politicos and the royals. Are they fair-minded? Do they think of the country first and not their own pocketbook?"

"Yes, certainly, there are many who do." At her arch look, he forced himself to be honest. "And many who do not."

"There it is," she said firmly. "A few honorable gentlemen shall be the hope for us all."

"Well," he said dryly, "perhaps it will be different in the Galapagos."

She laughed, the sound sweet to his ears. "I am sure it is."

They rode in silence then. The traffic was clogged, the stench even worse. But she seemed content to look at the fading sunset and dream of an island far away. What kind of life was it where a girl's fantasies took her to something so far removed from reality? A prince in the Galapagos instead of a baker's son right here.

"You must look around you, Amber," he said, daring to use her given name. "You must try to live in the world we have, and not in one that can never be."

She looked at him, surprised. "Why?"

"Because we cannot change what is here unless we set our thoughts here."

"I am an immigrant who works nightly in a gambling den. I cannot change anything, and so I shall dream of there, wherever it might be."

He could not argue that. Thanks to the circumstance of his birth, he had every advantage. Who was he to judge how she spent her days? And yet, he wished she had better. Better prospects, better circumstances, a better life.

But all he could do was give her a couple nights with his sister and a ball where she might indeed dance with a prince. Well, probably not a prince, but definitely an earl, for he meant to claim at least one set from her hand.

"Do you know how to waltz?" he asked abruptly.

She blinked in surprise. "No. The dance master considers it too scandalous."

"Ask Diana to teach it to you, then save the first one for me."

She nodded slowly, her eyes huge. He smiled at her then, knowing that at this moment, her thoughts were not on some island prince but of him and her dancing a scandalous dance. Her face brightened, and he saw the pulse in her neck leap in anticipation. If it were a different circumstance, he would steal a kiss. Sweetly at first, but with increasing passion, until he was the one reading her poetry at her bedside and singing arias to her as she slept.

Caught in such sweet imaginings, they traveled in silence to her home.

CHAPTER SEVEN

AMBER'S FATHER DID not approve, but he was reassured when Lord Byrn told him the head bouncer, Titan, would provide a couple extra footmen as her escorts. Amber guessed they were really there to protect Diana from her stepson, Mr. Geoffrey Hough. That detail didn't matter to Amber or her father. They all knew the men would look after Amber as well.

Which is how, exactly one day later, she was standing outside of Lady Morthan's home, waiting to be announced into the ball. Excitement seemed to crackle in the air as she drew in every breath. She couldn't keep her feet still. This was going to be the best night of her life, and she couldn't wait for it to begin. She kept shifting from one leg to the other while Diana smiled indulgently at her.

Diana's mother was with them as well, chattering about her old friends from school and how each of them was a viper who had betrayed her in one way or another. Last of their party was Lord Byrn, still in black but somehow managing to look magnificent.

"I keep telling you, Mama," Diana said, "Amber is the sister of one of *my friends*. Elliott got it wrong."

"I am so sorry, Mother," Lord Byrn intoned.

"Well, I don't see how she can just show up and—"

"It was the mail, my lady," Amber interrupted. "My letter must have gotten lost. That sort of thing happens all the time on the Continent."

It wasn't true, as far as she was aware, but Lady Byrn seemed to enjoy talking about how everything *over there* was worse than it was *here*. And sure enough, she began to expound on all the things that someone had told her simply did not work on the Continent. Which left Amber free to look at everything and everyone.

At first, she feared that some of the ladies who frequented the Lyon's Den would recognize her, but so far, none were in attendance. It was the gentlemen who posed the real threat. Nearly every man here had visited the place at one time or another, but she had been a nameless, faceless woman who helped her grandfather set a value on their goods. Surely they wouldn't recognize her?

She bit her lip, flinching away from one of the biggest louts who frequented the Den. And as she turned, her gaze connected with Lord Byrn's. Apparently, he'd been watching her as closely as she'd been looking around. Then as their gazes connected, his expression softened.

"Have I told you how exquisite you look tonight?" he asked.

She was wearing a pale yellow gown of an old style, quickly resewn to her body. The trim had been removed, a bit of ribbon added, and the sleeves changed. All of that in a day, such that every inch fit her like a dream. Even with the pale color, she felt like sunlight personified. When she'd first put it on, Diana had made her twirl around to show off every angle, and Amber had laughed like she hadn't since she was a child.

"The clip in your hair. Is the lion of your own design?"

"Yes," she said. She'd made it as well. It was meant to be a gift to Mrs. Dove-Lyon for next Christmas, but she hadn't been able to resist wearing it now. The burnished gold matched her gown, and the bright, ruby eyes would dance in the candlelight.

"Of her own design?" Lady Byrn asked. "How could that be?"

"It is a hobby of hers, Mother," Lord Byrn responded. "I have seen her sketchbook filled with jewelry designs. It is quite impressive."

"Really?" the lady asked. "Could you fashion a peacock for my hair? With beautiful plumage to trail down my face."

"It would be my absolute pleasure." Not a lie. It would be a gloriously fun thing to do. "And while I am in London, I shall look for a good jeweler who could bring the design to life for you." Especially since the thing would cost the moon and would amply repay her father for the two night's he'd have to spend in the cage with her grandfather in her stead.

"Hmm," Lord Byrn drawled. "I wonder what jeweler you will pick." He didn't sound upset by that. More amused than anything else. "Keep the design modest, please. We aren't made of gold."

"But the peacock will be. And it shall look wonderful in your mother's hair."

Lady Byrn preened at the thought. With Amber's help, she began to speculate on what gemstones could be in it. And so, they progressed up the line inch by slow inch. The anticipation was killing her, but talking about jewelry was the best way to pass the time, especially as Lady Byrn began pointing out what the other ladies wore. It was the kind of discussion that would be invaluable to her later. It told her what society women wanted, what styles they preferred, and what was seen as too much or too little.

If only she could focus on it rather than the approaching door. She could hear the Major Domo announcing everyone as they entered. Lord and Lady Castlereagh stood out in her mind. Imagine, she was about to be at a ball with such an important man! And if the jewelry was anything to judge by, she was surrounded by unimaginable wealth. It would have made her feel self-conscious if she hadn't known her own design matched theirs in skill. Plus, Lord Byrn was by her side, making her feel safe as he smiled warmly at her whenever she glanced his way.

"First balls are so exciting," Diana whispered in her ear. "I'm so happy to be here with you."

She grabbed Diana's hand and gripped it tight, then watched as Lord Byrn extended his arm to his mother. Now that was an impressive sight. The man was handsome with his broad shoulders and dark clothing. Amber pretended he was offering to escort her. She watched as Lady Byrn set her fingertips on his forearm, straightened her shoulders, and stepped forward as if she were the queen.

They were introduced with a booming voice, and all heads turned to see them enter. Then with stately movements, they descended the stairs just like royalty.

"Our turn," Diana whispered. "Head high."

Amber soothed out her gown, took a deep breath, and then at Diana's urging, linked arms with her. They stepped up and were announced.

"Lady Dunnamore! Miss Amber Gohar!"

Her name. Out loud. At a ball!

No one looked. Or at least not many. But it didn't matter, because at the base of the stairs, after the receiving line, Lord Byrn had stopped to await them. Lady Byrn had already wandered off to talk to her friends, but her son stood there and watched. His expression was genial, but his green eyes met hers with an intensity that made her heartbeat accelerate. And it was already going so fast.

Lord Byrn held out his hand to her. To her! She took it, and he helped her down the last step. Then he waited as she made her curtsey to Lady Morthan and the rest of the receiving line before escorting her into the ballroom proper. He set her gloved hand on his forearm, and he even squeezed it a bit, which set butterflies dancing in her belly.

"What would you like to do first?" he asked. "Lemonade? A turn about the room?"

"Wait, wait," Diana said as she held up three dance cards. "Put this on your wrist," she said to Amber. "You have a pencil in your reticule, yes?"

She did, along with a piece of paper, so that she could sketch the brooch.

"And I brought one as well." Lord Byrn pulled out a small pencil from his pocket and took the dance card from his sister's hand. "If I may?" he asked Amber as he held his pencil aloft.

It took a moment for her to understand that he was asking her permission to write his name on her dance card. Asking for her permission as if she were someone special.

She tried to swallow the lump in her throat and barely managed a nod. She watched in stunned delight as he scrawled his name for the first dance and the first waltz. Two dances with him! She would not be a wallflower this night. Well, at least not the *whole* night. Then she held out her hand as he tied the card around her wrist.

"I know it's not the same as your own ball, but I shall be very pleased to escort you out for your first dance."

She felt like she would burst from happiness. "Thank you," she whispered. She meant so much more than those two words, but it would have to do.

"And what of me?" Diana said, her voice teasingly sharp. "Am I to sit with the old ladies all night?"

"They shall be lining up for you, Diana. You know they will. But if I could beg the second waltz, would that be enough?"

"Definitely not. I shall have the second dance with you after Amber." Then she held out her card, and he dutifully wrote his name. "Don't forget, Mother will want your attendance as well. Not to mention—"

"I know my duties, sister dear." Then he turned to Amber. "Speaking of which, shall we walk?" At her surprised look, he tilted his head. "The portrait is over there."

Ah yes. The reason she was here. He wanted to be sure she sketched the brooch. The light dimmed from her heart. It was the perfect reminder that she wasn't here as an honored guest, but as a fraud here to sketch a design.

"Of course," she murmured.

"I'll be off then," Diana said. "Amelia's over there, and I haven't spoken with her in ages."

So it was just the two of them walking slowly through the ballroom toward a portrait. "Lady Morthan is known to stint on her spirits, but the lemonade is passable. As is the midnight buffet. But don't eat the shrimp, it made half the *ton* sick last year."

Shrimp? Spirits? "I shall follow your lead," she finally said. Especially since she'd never had spirits, mostly because the example of drunken men in the Den had never left her with a desire to taste it. As for shrimp, that was something the aristocrats ate. She lived on meat pies and black bread, though she had snuck a taste of crab once from Mrs. Dove-Lyon's buffet. It had been Christmas, and the lady had made enough that the staff was allowed a small taste.

"Now tell me what you are most excited about tonight. Is it the dancing? The food? The fashion?"

It was all of the above, but she didn't get a chance to answer. He hadn't even finished his questions when a portly gentleman stepped into their path. "Byrn, wasn't sure if you'd be here tonight."

"I'm dancing attendance on my mother. May I introduce you to my sister's dear friend, Miss Amber Gohar."

"Enchanted, m'dear," the man said as he bowed quickly over her hand. She thought he said his name, but it was lost because his mouth was at her glove. Then he straightened and went right back to his conversation with Lord Byrn. "We need to discuss this resolution of yours. You can't mean to spend that much on the veterans. There are other places that need the money more."

"I do mean to spend every ha'penny on our soldiers. They deserve it and..."

The discussion continued for long minutes. And though she did get a quick understanding of his resolution and the objections to it, she did not get a chance to speak or do anything but stand there feeling stupid. What did she know of governing? Not a thing, not that anyone was interested in her opinion anyway.

"I have promised Miss Gohar some lemonade," Lord Byrn eventually said.

"Quite right, quite right. I do hope you enjoy the ball, Miss Gohar." And then just before they were to move on, he pulled out a pencil. "Nearly forgot. Must have a dance with someone as lovely as you. With your permission?"

Was he asking to dance with her? Apparently so, because he was already grabbing at the dance card on her wrist. She obliged him by lifting it up, and he scribbled his name on the next open line.

"Charming," he said when he was done, and it took another moment for her to realize that it was his way of dismissing them. He turned immediately to scan the crowd before heading off in another direction.

"Don't worry," Lord Byrn said in her ear. "He's a decent dancer. Won't step on your toes."

She hadn't been worried until now. "I just hope I can remember the steps." She was pretty sure she could, but then she'd never danced at a real ball before.

"I have every confidence—" he began, but a pair of gentlemen turned in their direction and spoke over his words.

"Byrn, hello there! Doing the pretty for your mother and sister?"

"And my sister's dear friend. Gentleman, may I present Miss Amber Gohar."

"Enchanted," they said in unison. They bowed over her hand while Lord Byrn gave their names.

Each begged permission and then wrote their names next to dances, but their attention remained on Lord Byrn and politics. A different resolution this time. They were asking for his support, and Lord Byrn wasn't as committed. The discussion lasted no more than three minutes, but then there were more gentlemen, more discussions, and more names upon her dance card. At least some of the men had ladies upon their arm. The women looked vaguely bored as they, too, were introduced, then held up their cards. Lord Byrn wrote his name and then paused long enough to record the lady's name in his card.

In truth, there was a lot more writing and recording than she'd ever expected at a ball. And now that she was here, there were a lot of things that she hadn't anticipated but saw as completely logical.

In her daydreams, she'd only thought of the dancing, but now she saw the business of the ballroom. All over were ladies standing in small groups, while the men approached. It didn't take much to realize these ladies were searching for husbands. The men looking for wives went there and not to Amber. Older women sat in a clutch to one side, and men uninterested in the proceeding disappeared into what she guessed was the game room. Meanwhile, yet more gentlemen—the politicals if she were to guess—were busy greeting one another before leaping to whatever issue was important to them. Corn, finance, veterans. She had no understanding of it all, but Lord Byrn handled it with ease.

"Forgive me, gentleman, but I see Lady Castlereagh and must present Miss Gohar."

The gentlemen faded away, and just as Amber was turning toward the portrait hung close by, his words finally registered. Lady Castlereagh? And he meant to present her? "What are you doing?" she asked, aghast. She was a tradeswoman. She couldn't meet one of the reigning patronesses of society! Even she had heard of the ladies who ruled Almack's with an iron hand.

But there was no time for it as Lord Byrn was bowing over the older lady's hand. "You look quite lovely this evening," he said. "May I present to you my sister's dear friend, Miss Amber Gohar from Berlin? She is in town visiting for a time."

Amber dropped into a curtsey while the woman frowned. "Gohar? Do I know that name?"

Good God, she hoped not! Could her father's scandal have followed her here? Now?

"I doubt it," Lord Byrn was saying. "She is from a small but respectable family. You know the Germans. Every family has a connection to some prince somewhere. But Miss Gohar is a delight and most welcome in our home."

"Your sister's friend, you say?"

"From school. Forgive me, but I can't remember the specifics."

Amber mentally scrambled for details. What would she say should the lady ask? But she was spared her lies as Lady Castlereagh tsked in the way of a fond aunt.

"Men never remember the important things." She blew out a breath. "Very well. I suppose you have come to ask that she may waltz."

Lord Byrn flashed a charming smile. "They are dancing it already on the Continent."

The lady pursed her lips in thought while Amber's pulse beat rapidly in her throat. She needed permission to dance the waltz? She hadn't known. And already there were names on her card next to the scandalous dance. What if she was denied permission? What if—

"It is good to see your sister out again in society. Does she fare well? I hear her husband has fallen ill."

"Yes, I'm afraid that's true. In fact, I believe she would have remained at his bedside if it were not for Miss Gohar's presence."

"Hmm." The woman looked at Amber again, and this time her inspection was quite thorough. She seemed to study everything from Amber's head down to her slippered toes, her gaze lingering on the flaws in the rapidly remade gown. At least in Amber's mind, she did.

"That is an interesting design in your hair piece. Family crest?"

The lion? "Of a sort, my lady." Thank God she wasn't stammering, though it was a near thing. "It is a beast that means a great deal to my family. It symbolizes courage in uncertain times."

"Yes, yes. Though not quite as uncertain as it once was, now that the Corsican is gone."

"Quite right," Lord Byrn said.

Napoleon was defeated, and the world was returning to some form of normalcy. At least that's what Amber assumed they meant. Politics had never been of much interest to her, and yet among these people, it was their daily fare. After all, they were the ones running the country, and she was no one at all.

"Very well, Lord Byrn, she may dance," Lady Castlereagh said loudly. "Provided I see you at Almack's in two days." She arched a brow. "Have we a bargain?"

"We do," he said as he bowed over her hand. And as he did so, the lady shot a look at Amber.

"You are welcome as well. I shall see that the vouchers are sent."

What? Her in Almack's? The haven of the most proper, most elite ladies of the *ton*? Amber waited until they were just beyond earshot before she spoke, her voice squeaking slightly in alarm.

"I can't go to Almack's!"

Lord Byrn exchanged a nod with another gentleman, but his words were for her. "Whyever not? It's just her way of getting me to the marriage mart. There's nothing sacred about that place. Quite the opposite."

Of course, there was nothing special about it. *To him.* But she'd been hearing tales of the place since she first started helping the dance master at the Lyon's Den. The girls who came there spoke of an Almack's voucher as if they were describing a royal decree. And Amber had daydreamed the missives into an elaborate gold envelope with a blood-red seal. The paper was the whitest linen ever made, and every stroke of the pen was beautiful in curve as it was in content.

She was to receive one of those missives! Sweet heaven, she was giddy with delight. Until Lord Byrn realized what they were discussing and why she'd said she couldn't go.

"Oh, right. That's in two days, and our business will be done by then." He pursed his lips. "I suppose I can fashion some excuse for you. I'll have to go, but you needn't be bothered."

Bothered? Bothered! The man didn't understand anything at all. She'd give her right hand to attend. But before she could speak, they came to the portrait. The one of Lady Morthan in her youth as she wore the brooch Amber was supposed to copy.

And that, it turned out, was an utter disaster.

CHAPTER EIGHT

"I T WON'T WORK."

Elliott jolted at the sound of Amber's words. They were spoken low, but the misery in them was palpable. "What? Why not?"

"Look at it," she said as she gestured at the portrait of the young Lady Morthan at her presentation.

He was looking. He saw the brooch clear as day. A square-cut ruby surrounded by diamonds.

"Can you tell if the ruby has a bevel setting, or is it pronged?"

He didn't even understand the words, but it didn't matter. "It's a smear of red."

"Exactly. I can recreate the general idea, but anyone who knows the piece will be able to tell it's a fraud."

Oh hell. The whole scheme was dependent upon the countess not knowing exactly what her feckless grandson had done. And if there was one thing the lady knew, it was her jewelry.

"Is there another portrait?" she asked.

"None that I am aware of. But perhaps Lord Morthan knows of one." He rubbed a hand over his jaw. "He's here somewhere. Probably at the sideboard drinking all the port." And how had his life become so deuced ridiculous that he was searching a ball for a man who might help him forge a piece of jewelry, all because the country had forgotten to care for its own soldiers? "Come along. I'll walk you back to my sister. Did you want some lemonade before I return you?"

She blinked, her eyes wide with hope as she spoke. "I can stay?"

He frowned. "Stay? Stay where?"

"Here. At the ball. Even though I can't make the brooch."

"Of course, you can stay. What kind of man would I be if I took away your fun simply because my plans didn't work out?"

She didn't answer, but then again, she didn't need to. The only men of his set she knew were the ones who frequented the Lyon's Den. Not the best examples of humanity, by his standards, and so he lifted her hand and bowed over it.

"It should be my greatest pleasure to allow you to stay until the candles are blown out, and your feet ache abominably."

"Thank you," she said, her voice a bare whisper. "My lord, I cannot express—"

He waved her to silence as he took her arm. "Come on. Let us try Lady Morthan's minimally acceptable lemonade."

She gave him a dazzling smile, set her hand on his arm, and hopped twice on her tiptoes as they walked. And he nearly copied her, because he was pleased to see her so happy.

The evening's agenda was set. She was to have a marvelous time, and he was to do what he always did at these affairs. He danced where he ought, discussed where he needed to, and watched the clock for the minute he would be able to escape the ladies in favor of the more serious-minded work of running the country. Except this time, instead of watching the clock, he watched her.

It was a pleasure to lead her out for her first set, to feel her fingers grip his, and to see how easily her body moved through the dance steps. But then the dance was over, and he had to watch while another man drew her to the floor, looked into her bright eyes, and spoke of whatever nonsense had her smiling. And then another and another.

He watched with growing impatience until the first waltz, which was hard to do given that he was attending to his mother and sister, not to mention all the hopeful ladies who had his name on their dance cards.

"What has you scowling so fiercely?" his sister chided. "Is it that law for the soldiers?"

"Yes," he lied. "I have had a setback."

"Does it have anything to do with the mysterious Miss Gohar?" she asked. "You seem to be frowning at her quite often."

Had he? At her dancing partners, more like, but he couldn't say that to his sister. She would start to get all sorts of errant thoughts. "She is not the cause of the problem," he said honestly, "but the solution, I hope." He all but growled as a young heir to a worthless title bowed over her hand. The idiot would eventually have a vote in the House of Lords, so it was useful to be polite to him, but that didn't mean the twit should slobber all over Amber's hand as he bent to kiss it.

"Then, I hope you will remember that we are at a ball, and you are to make merry, not make morbid."

It took him a moment to hear what his sister said. And then he turned to her with a frown. "What?"

She rolled her eyes. "Come now. I haven't seen you this grumpy since Gwen threw your first speech into the fire."

"She called it ludicrous!"

"No, she called you ludicrous. She called your speech twaddle."

Sadly, Gwen had been absolutely right. In fact, her destruction had saved him from making a fool of himself before the House of Lords. "Gwen was being mean," he finally said.

"That still doesn't explain why you're scowling now. And look, now you've forgotten you're supposed to partner with Miss Cork."

"What? Damn." His sister was correct, and there was poor Miss

Cork staring at him as if he'd just murdered her dog.

Bowing his goodbye to his sister, he hurried over to the neglected lady and tried to make up for his mistake. He did a poor job of it, and while he tried to tease her into forgiving him, his gaze kept wandering back to Amber.

She did look lovely in that gown, but it was the lion in her hair that drew the eye. Unless, of course, one wished to look at her face. At the sweet curve of her cheek or the impish shape of her nose. Was that her laugh, dancing above the notes of the orchestra? Or had he completely lost his mind? What was he doing thinking such things of a trades-woman who was simply a means to getting his resolution passed? Albeit a fascinating tradeswoman with a laugh that made his heart lighter at the sound.

He resolved to think no more of her but failed completely at that. And then, finally, it was time for their waltz. He should have claimed all her waltzes, but that would have set tongues to wagging. He had to be content with this one dance when he could pull her into his arms. She stood stiff at first, and she bit her lower lip as if she were nervous. But then he squeezed her hand, and her gaze shot up to his.

"My lord?"

"Do you know why I love the waltz?"

She shook her head. "I only learned it a few hours ago."

He smiled. The orchestra was starting. "It's because I can do this." He tightened his grip, and he started moving them around the dance floor.

It took her a moment to settle in. Dancing required strength—of which she had a great deal—and trust—which he had to seduce her into giving him. He did that by smiling at her, by getting lost in the light in her eyes, and by knowing he was the perfect guide in this. He knew how to hold her, how to match his steps to hers, and how to time his breaths so they flowed together.

It was exhilarating. Not just the dance, but the way she slowly surrendered to him. By the end, her head was tilted slightly back, her hips were nearly touching his, and they moved like they were flying.

Then the music ended, and they slowed to a stop. He held her still, looking down at her. Her cheeks were flushed, and her lips parted to release an ecstatic sigh. She would look this way after lovemaking, he realized. Only she'd be naked, and he would be seated inside her.

The idea made his body tighten with hunger as lust surged through his blood. But he didn't act on it. He didn't even move. He just stared at her and yearned for something more. He *wanted* her.

He could seduce her. There were ways. She wasn't a gentlewoman, and the consequences for him would be minor despite the threat from all those protectors of hers. She would keep it secret from them if she enjoyed it. If she wanted it as much as he wanted her. Plus, he could make it worth her while financially. But the idea was heinous, and he was ashamed of himself for even thinking it. And yet, she stood there like temptation incarnate, and he was not at all sure he would refuse.

The couples broke apart, and a new set was forming. He had another dance partner, as did she. He released her hand and waist, but he didn't step back. He couldn't force his feet to move. Not until he was jostled aside by her next partner and nearly fell sideways into his own.

It took an act of will for him to drag his mind away from her and focus on the woman before him. And then he had to keep doing that as Amber danced the night away. She even had a different partner for the midnight buffet. In the end, he had to remove himself from the situation entirely. He stepped into the card room, and though he didn't play, he listened to the gossip and tried to drum up support for his resolution.

It didn't work. He couldn't focus. So, he went back out into the ballroom and danced with every wallflower there plus a few of the matrons. Every girl who was not the one he wanted, until finally, blessedly, the evening was done.

He gathered Amber from her last dance partner and set her arm upon his forearm as if he were tethering her to him. "Did you have a good evening?" he asked.

"Oh, yes," she breathed. "Though you were right. My feet hurt abominably."

"It takes endurance to dance all night."

She nodded. "But I don't want it to end."

Neither did he, though he could wish that they occupied themselves in other ways than here. More private, personal ways.

"Where are your sister and mother?" she asked.

"They left hours ago. Diana to see how her husband fares, and Mother to a different ball."

"There was another?" she asked.

"Scores. Mum usually goes to three in an evening."

"Three?" she gasped as she pressed her palms to her flushed cheeks. "I can't imagine that many in one night. One was more than enough."

One woman could be enough if it were her in his bed. Tonight. Every night. The lust was pounding in his blood as he gestured to the front door where a footman waited with her cloak. "I'm to escort you home."

"You? Alone?" She frowned. "Is that proper?"

Of course not. Especially since he was thinking of all the things to do to her in a closed carriage. "I won't tell if you won't."

She smiled at him and shook her head. "I suppose it doesn't matter anyway." She lowered her voice and giggled. "I'm not a respectable woman."

He smiled as she drew on her cloak, hearing her laughter echo in his thoughts. "How much champagne did you drink?"

"None. I was too busy dancing. Every set, every waltz, every moment, just like you promised."

He had. And she had. And now he wanted her alone in his carriage, so they could do so much more. "This way," he said as he held out his arm.

She willingly took it, and for all that she claimed her feet hurt, she was half dancing down the walk to his waiting carriage.

"This was the best night of my life," she breathed. "Thank you for this. I know it wasn't meant as a treat for me, but I loved it."

"Of course, it was meant as a treat," he said. "Do you think I wait until nearly three of the clock for everyone? It was for you," he said against her ear. Then he helped her inside the dark carriage. He sat beside her and repeated it. "It was all for you."

He heard her gasp as the door shut behind him. He felt her leg tremble slightly against his as his coachman clucked to the horses. And then he felt her breath, high and tight, as she whispered into the dark.

"My lord?"

"Call me Elliott."

"I can't! That wouldn't be—"

"Just now. Here while we're alone."

Silence.

"Elliot."

Never had his name sounded sweeter.

"I want to kiss you," he said to the darkness. "If I promise not to touch anything more than your face, will you allow it?"

He heard her breath catch, and then he heard her soft exhale.

"Do you promise?"

Did he? Could he kiss her lips and not touch her breasts, her thighs, her sweet honey?

"Yes," he said. "Unless you ask for more."

She gasped at his tease, and he was quick to reassure her.

"You are in control, Amber. Tonight is for anything you want." But the devil in him made him push her a bit more. "In fact, I give you leave to touch me any way you wish."

"I won't," she said. "I don't know how."

That was a declaration of innocence if ever he'd heard one. She might work nightly in an infamous gaming den, but she was still pure. That made him want her even more.

"One kiss then," he said. He reached out to caress her cheek and stroke his thumb down the long column of her neck.

"Or two," she whispered. "I might like two."

He grinned. "Two, then."

Then he took so much more.

CHAPTER NINE

AMBER HAD KISSED several men over her twenty-five years. Several meaning exactly seven, not counting her relatives. The upstairs ladies had been very forthcoming about exactly what was involved in sex. And they had explained what was good and not good in hilarious terms. So, every year on her birthday starting at the age of eighteen, the ladies had arranged for her to kiss a gentleman they described as one of the best.

Her conclusion after all that vast experience? She found kissing to be either too wet or too much mashing of teeth together.

Not true with Elliott. Perhaps it was because he didn't go straight to the kiss. He lingered in the dark, exploring her face with his fingertips, touching every inch of her cheeks, jaw, and even the slope of her nose. It made her giggle, and when she did, he released a sigh of delight.

"There it is. Like happiness wrapped up in sound," he whispered. Then he pressed his lips so close to her ear that she felt the heat of his breath. "Do it again," he urged.

"I can't giggle on command," she whispered back.

"Are you sure?" His finger traced down her nose once again.

She giggled at the feel. She giggled at the silliness of it all. And most of all, she laughed because he wanted her to. And as she relaxed, her head back, he shifted until his mouth teased hers. Just at the edge of her lips, and he rubbed back and forth across hers.

No one had done that before, and her mouth felt like it was swelling with the sensation. Then he surprised her by licking her top lip. A quick dart of his tongue and she gasped, her entire body tightening with excitement. She wanted to wait to see what he would do next, but every part of her was straining forward. If this was the prelude, what would the kiss be like?

Unable to wait a moment longer, she echoed his movement, licking his upper lip, and while he smiled in reaction, she pressed her mouth to his. His lips were lush, his mouth firm, and his tongue teased against hers, following when she retreated.

Then he took over. He filled her mouth, dueling with her, brushing against teeth and the roof of her mouth. She fell back against the squabs, letting him press against her. He was a large man, certainly compared to her, and she felt him everywhere and yet not close enough. Her hands had been by her sides, but now she gripped his arms as she clutched him tighter.

It went on for a glorious age, but eventually, she broke away as she gasped for breath. What an experience! And while she knew it was wrong, she ached for him to do it again and so much more. Her breasts felt heavy, her body hot with desire. She knew the stages of arousal in general terms. Suddenly, she felt them quite specifically. The tight pull of her nipples, the heaviness in her belly, and the wetness between her thighs. The upstairs girls hadn't said how delicious it felt.

"One," he rasped against her ear.

One what? Oh! One kiss. And she'd allowed him two, so there was more.

"Yes," she whispered.

He smiled. She could feel the curve of his mouth against her ear. "Have you ever been kissed before?" he asked.

"Yes."

"On your mouth?"

"Yes."

"Anywhere else?"

She swallowed. "No."

"Would you like to experience it?"

Yes! A thousand times, yes! But she couldn't say the words aloud. She could only nod.

He pressed his mouth to the bare flesh just below her ear. She felt the rough brush of his jaw against the curve of her neck.

"Has anyone ever kissed your breasts? Have you ever felt the quickening inside your belly?"

"No," she said again.

"I can show you. I can do it, and you shall remain a virgin. But you will know—"

"Yes!" she gasped. She had heard of such things from the upstairs girls, and she wanted to know.

He moved until he knelt on the carriage floor before her. He tugged her upright enough to unbutton her gown and ease it down her shoulders. Her corset was a short one, tied in front. He pressed his lips to the flesh above her chest, scraping his teeth across the skin before soothing it with his tongue. She felt him loosen the ties, and she took a deep breath that pushed the corset open. He tugged on the ribbons even more until it gaped in front and fell away.

Then his hands were on her breasts, kneading them in a way she had never thought to experience. Not like this. Not with every part of her body lifting with his movements while lightning shot from her nipples through her belly. He pinched her breasts, and she cried out in delight. She was overwhelmed with the sensations, and yet she wanted more and more.

"That is wonderful," she breathed. Then an imp inside her made her press him. "But it is not kissing."

"You want the kiss then?" he asked, his voice filling the darkness with a vibration she could almost feel. It teased her, and she ached to grab it, to hold it, and to let it caress every part of her.

"Very much," she answered.

"As you wish," he said, his lips barely grazing the flesh of her right breast.

She shivered with need. And then he made it even better as he used his teeth to tug at her nipple. Hot and quick while she lost control of her body. She arched and moaned. She spread her legs so that he could push closer. But he did not press closer. Instead, she felt his hand beneath her skirt, flowing upward over her knee and thigh, and bringing the hem of her skirt with it. Her legs were exposed to him, but in the dark, no one could see. Only feel. And she felt everything.

She might have said something, but she didn't have the breath. She might have asked, "What are you doing?" She might have said, "Whatever it is, do more. Do it again." But no words came, because he had moved to the other breast, laving it with his tongue, nipping at her with his teeth. The right breast was wet and cold, another feeling to contrast with the heat of his tongue on the other side.

"Do you like that?" he asked before he flicked his tongue up and down over her nipple.

Yes, yes, yes! Her mind was whirling, but she hadn't the strength to speak. Not until he paused. Not until his hands and his mouth stilled.

"Don't stop!" she said. Then she gripped his shoulders. "Please."

She felt his fingers slide higher between her thighs. He explored where she was wet. He stretched and teased, deep into her intimate flesh while she held her breath. And whenever he stilled, she called out to him.

"Please, more." She wanted to feel this. She wanted to know what this was like. "I have wanted to feel this for so long," she whispered.

"Please show me."

His fingers delved deeper until they opened her folds. And then he suckled again at her breasts. She was clutching his arm, squeezing her thighs together. But his chest was between her knees now. She was spread open as his fingers worked magic. They touched her, they circled, and they pressed deeper inside.

Nothing had ever been in there before. Certainly not a man with clever motions as he pushed in and out, in and out.

Her belly quivered, and she couldn't catch her breath.

His mouth left her breasts, and he stretched higher. His thumb was doing something, pressing somewhere that had her hips bucking. Harder. Faster. More! *Oh, please, more!*

"One last kiss," he whispered.

"Yes," she gasped. *Anything.* Because he had pushed his fingers deep into her while his thumb pressed against that other spot. Then he pulled back before doing it again.

A hard thrust of his hand.

"More," she pleaded as she arched into his palm.

Again. And again. Fingers rolling and twisting while his thumb—

Pleasure flooded every part of her body. His mouth slammed down on her cry.

Her body burst with waves of delight. Pulse after pulse, rolling outward from his hand.

He held her pinned like that, as she writhed in wonder. He kissed her quick and hard, muffling her sounds. Her hips moved as his hand did. In and out. In and out.

Too much! Don't stop!

Yes! Oh, beautiful, yes...

Until he stilled.

She was floating in bliss. His breath came in heavy pants against her cheek. He pulled his weight off her body and slowly withdrew his fingers from inside her.

"Your first quickening," he said. It wasn't a question, and she heard satisfaction in his tone.

"Is it always like that?"

He was silent a moment, then he said. "With me, it would be. If you wanted it."

She did. Right then, she wanted to do that over and over again, every night for the rest of her life.

He fell away from her, settling more comfortably on his heels. But her breasts were exposed in front of him, and he couldn't seem to leave them alone. Though one of his hands remained relaxed across her thigh, the other lifted her breast. It was a casual movement as if he wasn't even aware of what he was doing. But it made her want him again. She wanted everything again.

She didn't speak, and neither did he. In time, his other hand left her thigh to caress her other breast. She watched him, and what the darkness hid, she filled in with her imagination.

She saw his strong jaw, the straight line of his nose, and the luminous green of his eyes. She knew when his lips parted, and she felt the hunger in him.

"Be my mistress," he said. "Say yes to me."

"What?" His words were so rushed that she wasn't sure she heard him right. But then he explained, and she knew yet another shock on top of all the other surprises of the last two days.

"I can make it good for you. I can make you scream in pleasure every night. There's more to feel than what you had tonight. I can teach you."

His hand pushed quickly between her legs. She was already wet, much too sensitive, and yet he used the flat of his palm to push her open, and he rubbed in a circle over that spot.

Her belly tightened in reaction, and she cried out in alarm. But his other hand still held her breast, pinching her nipple again, and she began to tremble. It was good, and it was bad. It was wonderful, and it was too much.

"Feel this, Amber. Feel me."

She was! She was feeling nothing but him.

"Give it to me again!" he commanded. "Let me see."

He didn't cover her mouth this time. He didn't swallow her cry, but sat back and watched as her head arched back. As her thighs spread wide and she thrust into his palm.

"Now," he said as he rubbed hard against her. "Now." He did it again. "Now!"

Rapture burst seemingly from his mouth to her body. It had the feel of a piercing.

If she screamed, she didn't hear it. Sensation overwhelmed her. Then it carried her. And then she was simply there, her body splayed wide as the ripples continued, and he watched her.

"Say yes," he whispered. "Be my mistress."

"Mistress?" she echoed dumbly. *Not wife?*

"I cannot marry you," he said, his voice a low rumble. "My wife will be chosen for political advantage. She will advance my causes and train our children to do the same." He spoke in such a bloodless way, as if he selected his women by assets on a banker's sheet. "But my mistress will have more from me, and she can be anything I choose. I choose you, Amber. Say yes."

And be his mistress?

"No."

He had given her the best experience of her life. He had shown her things that she had always imagined, but never realized were possible for her. Not just here, but the whole night. She'd been to a ball. She'd danced with a baron, four future peers, and an earl. She'd stepped into his carriage and had felt such wonderous things.

But she knew when something was a dream. She was an expert at it. And she knew from listening to all the upstairs ladies that nothing true happens in a dream. In the morning, promises were never kept, wishes were never fulfilled, and the woman always paid in the end. Not the man with the luminous green eyes. Not the lord who could have any woman he wanted for the price of a smile. No, it was the woman who bore the disgrace and the baby, if there was one.

So she said, no, though the word hurt to say aloud. And when he looked at her with shock and disappointment, she knew she had chosen correctly.

Every man looked that way when denied a treat. When they lost at cards or learned their favorite girl was occupied with someone else. Just because Amber had been behind the cage didn't mean she was blind. She'd seen their faces, and she knew it took men less than an hour to turn their attention elsewhere.

Meanwhile, Elliott rocked back on his heels. And as he moved away, she was able to straighten up. Her knees closed, and she twitched her skirt down. She tugged awkwardly at the ribbons of her corset, ashamed that her hands were shaking.

He reached out, and she flinched from him. His eyes shot to hers, and maybe she saw hurt in them.

"You are safe with me," he said.

Was she? She didn't know. She felt so exposed.

"Hold the edges together. I will tie the ribbons."

She did as he instructed, holding the edges of her corset while he tightened the strings. Then he helped her with her dress, buttoning the back with practiced ease. And when it was all done, and he sat on the seat beside her, he rapped on the top of the carriage.

A muffled, "Yes, m'lord," was the response.

"Where are we going?" she asked, confused.

"To my sister's home, as I promised."

How long had they been driving? Shouldn't they be there by now? "Where have we been?"

"I don't know. A tour around Hyde Park most likely."

It took a moment for his words to filter in. A moment for her to realize that he had planned this. That he had prearranged with the coachman to ride them in a circle until their tryst was done.

"How many times have you done this before?"

He blew out a breath. "Never," he confessed. "You're my first." He sounded like she should be grateful to be treated like this. Like a common doxy tumbled in a carriage.

She wanted to be furious, except honesty forced her to admit that she had asked for it. She had *wanted* it. He had told her at the very beginning of their ride that he wanted to kiss her, but that it was her choice. And she had asked for two.

Her face burned with humiliation, and she wasn't fully aware of why. He was so much more worldly than she. Despite her talks with the upstairs ladies, she still didn't understand what had happened.

"Am...am I still a virgin?" she whispered.

"Yes. As respectable as ever." His voice was calm, and his matter-of-fact tone reassured her. Though, of course, a woman who worked in a gaming hell was not at all respectable. So even if he lied, she wasn't any worse off than before.

"You will tell no one?"

He stiffened in reaction. "I do not break my promises. I will tell no one." Then he paused. "Will you?"

"What? No!"

"No giggles between girls upstairs at the Den? No whispered confessions about the man you had on his knees before you?" There was a bitterness in his tone that rubbed against her raw nerves. He was angry with her, though he worked hard to hide it.

"Of course not. I don't break my promises, either."

"Good," he said as he adjusted his position on the seat. They were touching only slightly. His knee against her thigh. His hand on the back of the seat near her shoulder. Near, but not touching. Close, but not connecting. "I should like to see you tomorrow. Afternoon, if that's acceptable," he said.

"Of course," she said, feeling strange with his suddenly polite tone. "Whenever you like." She was, after all, staying with his sister. She hadn't the wherewithal to say no if he chose to visit.

"I have an idea for the brooch. I know the painting wasn't enough, but perhaps there is a way around that."

The brooch? The jewelry that had brought him into her circle in the first place. How fast this man thought. She was still reeling from everything, but his mind was back to his vote and the brooch he needed. "Whatever you think best. It is ample…" Her words cut off as she realized what she was about to say. But he was no fool. He finished it for her.

"Ample repayment for a ball and the ride home?"

He made it sound as if he were the upstairs person, and she the one demanding worship. There were a few upstairs men for such purposes, but she was not a customer. And she disliked the implication that what they'd just done was a transaction.

"I agreed to remake the brooch for you," she said tartly. "If you have found a way that I can do such, then I must perforce agree." She used her most educated voice merely because it made her feel more in control. "This evening was a lucky…" *Experience? Dream? Temptation?* "Happenstance. I am grateful for it." And she was thankful even though she felt as if she wanted to burst into tears. "The one—"

"Has nothing to do with the other?" He was silent for a long moment, and she used the time to gather her scattered wits. "Very well. I will speak no more of it." His tone held a strange note in it. As if he made fun of himself with his words. "And I apologize."

"For what?" she asked.

"For what, what?"

She huffed out in exasperation. "What do you apologize for? Men always say that without actually being sorry for anything."

He cleared his throat. "I apologize for taking advantage, Miss Gohar. I apologize for thinking you were one thing when you are decidedly not." There was definitely a wry note to his voice. "And I apologize for underestimating you."

Did she hear admiration in his tone as well? The idea made her lips curve in a wry smile. "You are not alone in making that mistake," she said. Most men underestimated a smart woman.

"I am not in the least bit surprised." Then he raised her hand to his mouth, bestowing the most courtly of kisses. "May I call upon you tomorrow afternoon?"

"Yes, my lord. I should be happy to see you then."

As if he had timed it specifically for this, the carriage rolled to a stop. They were at his sister's house. She did a last check of her hair and dress. Her hairpiece had fallen out, and she gasped as she tried to find the lion.

"Here," he said, handing it to her.

She took it from his hand, but he kept hold of it such that their fingers were entwined for a very long moment. She thought he would say something. She looked at his face and saw his mouth open, but no words came out. And in that awkward silence, the coachman opened the door.

That was enough to break the spell. Elliott released her hand and stepped out, only to turn and offer his hand again as she climbed out. It was all very polite, and every motion had been lived a million times in her imagination. A gentleman handed her out of the carriage and walked her to the front door. But never in her wildest dreams had she conceived of the reality of it. That the walk was nothing compared to what the ride had been. That the polite bow at the end of the night was nothing compared to what they had done in the dark.

"Good night, Miss Gohar," he said after the butler had opened the door.

"I had a lovely evening, Lord Byrn. Thank you."

Then he turned and walked away while the butler took her cloak from her shoulders. The door shut, and she heard the rumble as the carriage rolled away. The evening was done, and she had no idea how to feel about that.

She went to her room, undressed with the help of Diana's very sleepy maid, climbed into bed, and remembered. And tonight, unlike every night before, there were no fantasies at all. Only remembering. And curiosity about what would happen tomorrow.

CHAPTER TEN

AMBER WOKE LATE, which wasn't surprising given that she'd stayed up until dawn remembering her evening. But even after being awake all night, she couldn't stay in bed. Not when his lordship was coming to see her again this afternoon. Not when she was nervous and excited about all the things that might happen.

She knew none of them would. Today they were back to being aristocrat and merchant. He had a plan for how to get the brooch he needed. She had to return to her cage where she dreamed of lovely things but never lived them. Except, of course, for one wonderful night when she had.

She hummed as she dressed.

Until the moment she opened her bedroom door and there, lounging against the wall, was a large man with a dour look, dark circles under his eyes and a maimed hand. "Titan!" she gasped as she jerked backward in surprise. "What are you doing here?"

He was in charge of the bouncers who guarded the doors at the Lyon's Den. He'd been wounded at Waterloo like so many others, but since he was an officer and a natural leader, Mrs. Dove-Lyon had set him in charge of the others at her establishment. He was kind in a gruff way, and Amber liked him. The other girls adored him because many had reason to be grateful for his help at one time or another.

"I'm called Lucifer here," he grumbled.

What? But she didn't get a chance to ask as he pushed off the wall to tower over her. He was a tall man, and she had to fight her instinct to cringe away. Especially as he spoke, his words clipped and angry.

"I know how late you came back last night."

"I was at—"

"I know your hair was down, your face flushed, and your dress mussed."

Um…really?

"And I know that you took several circles around Hyde Park."

Oh, no.

"I am five and twenty, Titan—"

"Lucifer!" he snapped.

Right. "Lucifer, then. I am able to make my own choices."

He touched her chin, tilting her face up until she looked him in the eyes. "Did he take advantage of you?" There was a growl to his words that made her shudder in fear. He was angry, but maybe not at her.

"No," she rasped. "He did not take advantage."

Silence while her face heated.

"Then, you allowed it." His voice was low, but the violent edge was stronger.

"No!" she gasped. "Well, yes. A little. I… He…" *Oh, my.* His face was purpling in rage, but no more than hers was burning. She took a deep breath and invested strength into her words. "He asked, and I said no."

"He asked!" The two words came exploding out of him, and though anybody else would have run away, she was used to loud men. Bellows of whatever emotion rarely rattled her.

"All men ask!" she retorted. "Unlike others, he accepted my answer."

Titan…er, Lucifer's eyes widened. "But you allowed him. You

said—"

She sighed. "A little, yes. I'm five and twenty. Surely I'm allowed a kiss or two? You know where I work. You know that I'm not respectable."

"On the contrary," he responded. "I know exactly how respectable you are. Thisbe, there are any number of good men who would offer you marriage. Lysander and Demetrius—"

"Look more at my jewelry than they do at me," she said. At least she knew Lord Byrn wanted her for herself and not her family's business.

Lucifer sighed. "There are others who know the truth about you. Do not throw your lot in here." He gave an expansive gesture that was meant to encompass what? The entire house? The *ton*? "They do not play by the same rules," he said, his voice heavy.

She knew that. Didn't she see them every night gaming at the tables or taking their pleasure from the upstairs girls? She shook her head about to say that she would make her own decisions. That she already knew all his warnings and had made the right choice last night. But this morning, her heart was singing another tune. Lord Byrn was coming to the house to see her. Her heart wanted to perform arias on the rooftop.

She never got a chance to voice her thoughts as Diana's voice filled the hallway.

"What is the meaning of this?"

Both she and Lucifer jumped at her sharp tone. Diana was a petite woman, but her voice could cut as sharp as a knife. Lucifer sketched a bow.

"My lady—"

"Footmen do not belong up here, Mr. Lucifer. And they certainly don't harangue guests."

"Just Lucifer," he ground out. "And Miss Gold—"

"Gohar!" Amber hissed.

"Miss Gohar and I are well acquainted."

"I do not care if you have been raised from the cradle together." Diana stepped right up into his face. She could do that because he was still dipped in his bow, but the moment he stood, she was dwarfed by his size. And apparently not in the least bit intimidated. "You will not speak to my guest, you will not come to the upper floors unless requested, and you will not stand there like you belong here no matter what my brother has told you!"

Ah. There was the real problem. Lord Byrn had taken it upon himself to make changes in his sister's staff. An excellent idea, by Amber's reckoning, because Diana's horrible stepson did not make idle threats. But Diana was obviously used to defending her position in the house and did not take kindly to the intrusion. That it helped keep Lucifer away from Amber was a side benefit.

Lucifer sketched another bow, not so much insolent as indulgent. As if he were giving way to a petulant child. "You will see no more of me this day, my lady." Then he looked at Amber, and his expression was dark and unreadable. "Watch yourself, Miss. This is not your place."

"I decide if this is her place," Diana snapped. "She is welcome here, ergo—"

He shot a look at Lady Dunnamore. "Doesn't she return home today? Am I not supposed to drive her there after luncheon?"

Diana's eyes widened, and she looked at Amber. "You are leaving? I thought…" She swallowed. "I'd hoped you could remain for a bit longer. I received vouchers for Almack's an hour ago, and I've set Maddy to altering one of my gowns."

"Almack's?" Amber breathed. "Truly?"

"Truly. And you can't want to miss that."

She didn't. Never in a million years would she have thought to receive a voucher. The idea that she wouldn't be able to go broke her heart. But… "I believe my business with your brother is over," she finally admitted.

"Nonsense. You leave my brother to me. Besides," Diana said as she linked arms with Amber and drew her toward the stairs, "I want you to stay, and so you shall. I have need of a companion, and I find I like you quite well."

And wasn't that just like a peer to declare she wanted something and expect that everyone would comply? Except in this case, Amber wanted it with her whole heart. She just didn't know what her father and grandfather would do without her for so long. And if she doubted the wisdom of giving in to Diana, all she had to do was look behind her at Lucifer to see the grim way he was shaking his head.

She wasn't stupid. She knew she was allowing herself to be pulled into something that wasn't her life. Sleeping past noon, dresses given for free, and dancing at night. That life would never be hers. But if she viewed it as a holiday, it could be for a time. A few days of color in the midst of a lifetime of gray. What was the harm in that?

She resolutely turned her back on Lucifer and allowed Diana to pull her close. They went down to eat together, happily discussing dresses. Did she look better in a high cut gown? Did she prefer lace or ribbon? And how would her hair be styled? They spoke nothing of significance. No grand state of affairs and certainly nothing of the selling or buying of jewelry, which is what her father and grandfather always discussed. And yet, every word was gold to her. And when Diana showed her the voucher from Almack's, Amber traced the elegant sweep of her name on the linen. She stroked the edge of the paper and even brought it to her nose to catch the vague scent of rosewater. That last part could be imagined. There was no reason at all that Lady Castlereagh would drip rose scent upon a voucher. But in Amber's imagination, that little detail was added. As was the way she would dance yet another night through.

"Lord Byrn, my lady," her butler announced, jolting Amber out of her thoughts.

"Thank you, Simpson," Diana said. "Show him in here. And set another place at the table. My brother never remembers to eat."

Amber looked up from where she'd been stroking the voucher and imagining such things. Her heart was beating hard in her throat as she watched the door for Elliott to appear. In her dream, he would see her and light up with joy. He would grin, rush to her side, and drop immediately to his knee before her as he professed his love.

It was a ridiculous thought, and she mentally kicked herself for such an idea. But her imagination could never be restrained, only held up against reality to show her the truth.

Lord Byrn walked in wearing—no surprise—all black. His cravat was tied differently today, his hair mussed, and there were dark smudges beneath his eyes.

"Good heavens, brother," Diana cried. "You look positively haggard."

Her brother's eyebrows rose in surprise. "Surely not that bad." He kissed his sister's cheek then—far from dropping to one knee before her—he barely glanced at Amber before murmuring a polite, "Miss Gohar."

"Sit down. Eat. We have plenty here, and there's no reason for it to go to waste."

"You are too kind," Elliott said as he settled in a chair on the opposite side of the table as Amber.

"I know you too well," Diana said lightly. "Tell me what has brought you here so early."

Elliott didn't answer as the footman served him a hearty meal. He tucked into it with relish before shooting his sister a too innocent look. "How goes it with the new footmen?"

"Don't you mean spies?" she answered, her voice high.

Elliott's head and eyebrows lifted as he looked at his sister. He didn't speak, and neither did she until the silence stretched to an uncomfortable degree. And then she turned to the butler. "Thank you,

Simpson. I think we can manage from here."

"As you wish, my lady," the butler said as he gestured the footmen to precede him out of the room. He shut the door firmly behind him while Diana relaxed back in her seat as she regarded her brother. When she spoke, it was quiet, but her words hit with the force of a sledgehammer.

"Out with it, Elliott. Why am I hosting four new footman and a delightful new guest all from London's most infamous gaming hell?"

"My lady!" Amber gasped as she straightened out of her seat. She knew! She knew who Amber was, and she was not pleased.

"Sit down, Amber," Diana said gently. "I have no quarrel with you. I will delight in taking you to Almack's tomorrow. But the question— for my brother—remains. Why is everyone here?"

Elliott's brows drew down. "Almack's? Whyever would you want to go there?"

"Because she has a voucher, Elliott. And I shall be pleased to go with her, that's why."

Which was a lovely thought. It was a beautiful one! But not if Diana knew she was foisting a fraud into those hallowed halls. "I-I can't," Amber said as she fought the tears. "You know what I am."

"Do I?" Diana challenged. She arched a brow at her brother. "Who is she to you?"

The question was clear. Is she your mistress? And Amber would not sit down for that. "I make jewelry, my lady. I am the best there is in all of England, even though I am a woman. And it was not my choice to deceive you."

"Of that, I have no doubt," Diana drawled. Then she gestured at Amber's hair. "Did you make the lion you wore last night? It was exquisite."

Amber smiled and nodded. "I did. And Lord Byrn has asked me to make a specific piece based on—"

"That blighter, Larry John, sold Lady Morthan's brooch, and now if I am to get my resolution passed, I need the damned thing remade. It's been melted down, and Miss Gohar here is the only one I trust to remake it."

Diana frowned. "That ugly ruby thing? The one on the portrait they're so proud of?"

"Yes," Amber said. "Only it wasn't detailed enough."

Diana lifted her teacup to her lips. "Then have a look at the companion pieces. There's earbobs and a ring. Matches a neck pin her father used to wear."

Elliott nodded. "That was my thought exactly." He glanced at Amber. "You can deduce the design from those, can't you?"

She nodded. It should be enough. She hoped.

"Good. But the other pieces are at their country estate in a safe in his library. Deuced inconvenient, but I thought we would leave tomorrow morning early. We can be out there and back by nightfall."

So quickly. Her fun was ending so fast. "Yes, my lord—"

"You certainly cannot! Elliott, I told you. She has a voucher to *Almack's!*"

The man huffed out a breath but didn't argue. It was left to Amber to point out the obvious. "I'm a merchant, my lady. I cannot go—"

"You have a voucher, do you not?" She tapped her finger on the invitation.

"Yes, but—"

"And a sponsor, yes? I am here, am I not?"

For such a small woman, she could be decidedly imperious. "Yes, but—"

"Then you may go, and I will hear no more about it."

There was a long silence as both Amber and Elliott stared at her. It wasn't Amber's place to argue or even question, but she did. It wasn't in her nature to let something so bizarre go unchallenged. "*Why*, my lady?"

Diana set down her teacup with a hard click. "Do you know that it was Lady Castlereagh herself who convinced Mother to marry me to Lord Dunnamore?"

Elliott jolted. "What?"

"She and all the other ladies of Almack's came to see Mama. It was a tragedy, they all said. Papa dying so young and Mother so confused, but they had the solution."

"The devil you say," Elliott muttered.

"All of them came, but Lady Castlereagh was the one who spoke the most. She said that Mama wouldn't be able to handle things by herself. That she needed a man to help her."

Elliott pursed his lips. "She probably did. You know how..." He fluttered his hands about his head. "Distracted she can be."

"So, she agreed. Though she was still grieving Papa, she agreed to marry Lord Dunnamore."

"What?" Elliott asked, and no wonder. Because his mother had not been the one sacrificed to the altar.

"Lord Dunnamore didn't want her," said Diana. "Lady Castlereagh was most clear about that. He wanted someone young and tiny." She lifted her chin. "He wanted me, a girl not even out yet. And they were so firm that Mama agreed." She looked at her brother. "I stood at the top of the stairs and listened to it all. And then I stood there like an idiot, silent and miserable while they saw to my dress and the breakfast buffet. They managed the agreement between Mama and Lord Dunnamore. And they touted it as a great match, a great solution. Me, wed to a man three times my age. *They* did that to me."

Bitterness rang through her tone, and Amber bit her lip to keep from saying anything. What the ladies had done to the young Diana had been cruel.

"I failed you then, Diana—"

"No. You were much too young to know anything."

"But you cannot use Amber as they used you. She is not a weapon to wield against the Patronesses of Almack's in some twisted form of revenge."

Diana's brows rose as she looked at Amber. "You are a dignified, well-mannered woman," she said.

And how was Amber supposed to respond? "Thank—"

"You danced beautifully last night, and I heard not one word said against you. No one has heard of Miss Gohar, and no one questioned your story."

"That is my real name, my lady. We changed it when we came to England to fit in better."

Diana waved that comment away. "You are a jewelry maker, yes? So, your family has some money, I should think. Enough to dower you a little, at least."

She'd never asked her father that, but she assumed so. He had often talked of the diamond necklace her mother wore when they were wed.

"That puts you above more than half the maidens at Almack's. And if you, as a well-spoken and dowered young lady, were to meet a younger son or an heir in need of a dowered girl, then why shouldn't you dance together at Almack's? And why shouldn't you consider becoming the wife of such a man? Because you fashion jewelry? My father whittled little animals out of sticks. I embroider flowers upon chair cushions. Even Mama makes displays out of flowers."

"Those are not trades, my lady," Amber said, her voice barely above a whisper. "I am a tradeswoman."

"Why? Because you say so? I am fairly certain your father does not bandy it about that you fashion jewelry. I'd wager he claims it is done by his own hand."

Or her grandfather's trembling hand.

"So why then," continued Diana, "should it be wrong for a woman with a hobby to enter into the sacred Almack's halls? And if I, as a proper wife to my elderly husband, took pleasure in opening those narrow doors to deserving young ladies without a pedigree, then who is to say I am wrong?" She flashed her brother a truly devious smile. "That is not revenge, brother, that is social change."

Elliott stared at her, his jaw slack. And when it was clear that Diana would say no more, he leaned back in his chair. "My sister is a republican," he said, his voice hushed with shock.

"Oh, I shouldn't go as far as that," Diana said with a smile. "But I see no reason why a level-headed young woman should not be brought to Almack's to meet a husband to marry. And I shall be quite pleased to be the one to do it." Then she looked to Amber. "What say you? Shall you join me in a gilded cage? We can have tea and talk fashion to our heart's content. And then scheme to bring more deserving ladies into those very same halls as you will attend tomorrow night."

More deserving ladies? Like the upstairs girls? Like Lina, the mysterious Abacas Woman? The very idea was...interesting. And was exactly the kind of social change that Mrs. Dove-Lyon was trying to create. She daily tried to educate her girls into more refined manners and ways to be self-reliant. And the women who came to her asking for help in finding a husband were all of them blocked out of the proper course of things by the same kind of ladies as the Patronesses of Almack's. The women who sought Mrs. Dove-Lyon's help weren't of the right pedigree or fortune. They had been harmed by the men in their lives or cast aside by society in one way or another.

"I believe you and Mrs. Dove-Lyon would get along famously," Amber said softly.

"Don't be ridiculous!" Elliott said. "You will not go to a gaming hell!"

"Why not?" Diana winked at Amber. "I gather you go there quite often."

"I do," Amber said. "But if you wish to go, pray have me alongside you. Just as I shall be very pleased to have you with me at Almack's."

Diana clapped her hands. "Excellent! We have a bargain."

"We do not," Elliott declared, but no one was listening to him.

Amber and Diana were smiling at one another, and Amber's imagination had taken flight. Who might she dance with at Almack's? Just think of the eligible gentlemen she would meet and perhaps marry! The very idea brought her gaze back to Elliott. Because she was certain, he would not dance with her. And never, ever marry her. Hadn't he said that last night? And wasn't that reinforced now by the way he was scowling at his sister?

Clearly, he did not approve of her ideas on social change. And he certainly didn't approve of Amber dancing at Almack's or potentially marrying into his ranks. Which was like looking at a wet blanket on a dreary day. Even the sight of him depressed her.

"Do you know what I think?" Diana asked brightly.

Elliott groaned. "What now?"

"I think you should take Miss Gohar for a ride around Hyde Park this afternoon. If she is to be one of us, then she should be introduced properly, don't you think? And a tour about the park in the fashionable hour is just the way to show our support."

"But he doesn't," Amber pointed out as she looked at his stunned face. "He doesn't support me."

"He will," Diana returned archly. "He will if he wants me to keep Mr. Lucifer and all those new footmen running about."

"They're here to protect you," he grumbled.

"I have been protecting myself long before you came to London." Was there bitterness in her tone? Anger? Not exactly. More like resignation to her fate. But that didn't mean she'd lost her spirit as she boldly challenged her brother.

"Will you support her, Elliott? Will you help her marry well?"

Her brother swallowed the last of his tea, then looked to Amber. It was the first time this afternoon that he had set all his attention on her. And far from having a devoted expression, he looked as if he had just swallowed poison. "It shall be my pleasure to ride with you at the fashionable hour." His expression softened, and his words came out with sincerity. "But do you want to, Amber? Don't let my sister use you if this is not what you want."

"As opposed to how you are using me for your vote? And to dupe Lady Morthan into thinking her grandson isn't the grandest idiot of them all?"

He flinched, but he kept his expression clear. "Even so," he said. "I will only do this if you wish it."

"I do," she said with absolute truth. "I want to go to Hyde Park. I want to go to Almack's. I want to marry a young lord and leave my gray cage forever." She looked to Diana. "Even if I switch a gray cage for a gilded one, it is still an improvement. So yes, my lord, I shall be pleased to go riding with you."

"Excellent," Diana cried. "Now go away, brother. Amber and I have to discuss her wardrobe for this afternoon and then for tomorrow's dance." She winked at Amber. "And I shall talk to you about all the gentlemen who are likely to be present, who you should entertain, and who should be set aside like bad meat."

Amber thought she had better information on who was a bounder simply because she knew who frequented the Lyon's Den, but it was always good to know more. "I am at your disposal…Diana." It was bold of her to use the lady's given name after her deception had been revealed. But Diana smiled and then gave an arch look to her brother. "We shall expect you at four o'clock."

Her brother stood slowly as he stared at her. "You will allow Lucifer and his men to remain here? For as long as I deem it necessary?"

Diana froze a brief moment, but then she nodded. "Yes," she said softly. "I will allow it and…and attempt to be grateful for it."

Elliott gave his sister a bow. "Then, I am content. And I will see you this afternoon."

It was done. Amber's wildest dreams were coming true all because she was a convenient bargaining chip between brother and sister, not to mention an instrument of social change and possible revenge. None of that sat well. She was a person with desires of her own. But beggars couldn't be choosers, so she would take what she could and make the most of it.

And maybe, just maybe, she would meet her future husband today.

CHAPTER ELEVEN

POLITICS WAS A dicey game. Society was a great deal more complicated. And given that Elliott had spent the afternoon failing at the first game, he was not in the best frame of mind to attempt the second. But he had promised his sister, and so he appeared at her front door at precisely four of the clock. He was unhappy, frustrated, and not fit company for anyone. And yet, all of that disappeared the moment Amber stepped into the parlor.

She wore a simple gown of rose, too pale a color for her, he thought, but muted colors were expected of ladies entering the marriage mart. She smiled in greeting even as she turned to accept a fashionable wrap from his sister.

"This will keep you warm if the weather kicks up," Diana said. "But if you can stand it, keep it off. A little cold engages the male mind."

She meant that men enjoyed seeing the outline of nipples. If even the vaguest bumps appeared, men would come from everywhere just to greet her.

"She doesn't need ploys," Elliott grumbled as he shook out the wrap and put it across Amber's shoulders. "She's beautiful just as she is." He meant what he said to an almost disturbing degree. After all, he knew many lovely ladies, several of whom were considered quite beautiful. Objectively, Amber was fair but not exceptional.

Except when he looked at her, his breath was stolen away, and he couldn't figure out why. Her face was pleasing with clear skin and a pert nose. Her figure was delightfully curvy, but not overly so. Why was he struck dumb when she entered a room? And why did he watch as she murmured her thanks to the butler and smiled earnestly up at his sister?

Because she was honest, he realized. No coyness, no games. She looked directly at one when she spoke, and he saw no deviousness in her words or form. If she was embarrassed, he knew. And if she wanted something, he knew that as well. Her body was strong, telling him she labored. It didn't matter to him whether she was a farmhand or the grandest duchess in the land. She was not idle, and that appealed to him. But most of all, when she looked at him, he felt it. He felt her. Her attention, her perception, and even her desire.

He saw that all in her eyes and face when he offered her his arm. He felt her self-possession as they walked calmly toward his phaeton. And when he turned her around to lift her onto the seat, he felt her body tremble and saw her tongue dart out to wet her lips. That was desire, he thought. And it matched his own.

He set her on the seat but did not release her. "I don't like the idea of introducing you to other men. I don't like where this might lead."

She blinked. "You fear someone might recognize me?"

He frowned. In truth, the idea had never occurred to him. "Not at all. I don't want you looking at anyone but me." This was not an unusual thing to say among the *ton*. The flirts bandied about the phrase nearly every hour. But it was not typical of him, and he wondered if she knew that. Worse, he wondered what that meant for him. He was not a man to say silly things. He had more important worries on his mind. Affairs of state, the management of a nation. And yet, he was completely consumed by the idea that Miss Amber Gohar was shopping for a husband.

It upset him enough that he stomped his way around the phaeton before jumping up on the other side. Fortunately, she was still there, and this time her smile was teasing as her gaze locked with his.

"Will you feel better if I promise to look at you every moment we are together? At least one second for every minute."

He snorted. "And who shall get the other fifty-nine?"

"Someone who dresses with more flair," she responded tartly. "Like him, perhaps." She gestured across the street at Mr. Dennis Shaw. A young popinjay fresh out of school with more money than sense. Elliott wondered if the riot of colors in his attire made his valet physically ill.

"You cannot mean for me to dress like that."

She laughed, a truly lovely sound. "Not you. You haven't the mannerisms to carry it off. But he is worth a gander, don't you think?"

"Not even a gosling," he retorted as he got the horses moving. "I shudder to think what he paid for that monstrous attire."

"Enough to make the tailor very happy."

Well, he supposed he'd never thought of it that way. If Mr. Shaw had money to burn, then there were worse places to spend it than on a tailor who was feeding his family on the one purchase.

"You see," Amber said as she turned to look at him. "Fifty-nine seconds of incomprehensible color, and one second to rest my eyes with your unending, monotonous black." She frowned for a moment. "Did you wish to be a clergyman when you were a boy?"

"What? No! My fondest wish was to be a hussar. I wanted to ride a horse into battle with my sword flashing in the sun."

"Their uniforms are quite spectacular."

"Quite. I was a boy and easily impressed by such things." He shook his head. "I used to think military glory was the most exciting thing in the world."

"What changed you? I sincerely doubt you own a crimson coat or gold epaulets. Something happened to make you choose black, more black, and then a little white with your black."

"It wasn't ever the clothes that drew me. I wear black because it's convenient and doesn't show the dirt."

"Very practical," she agreed. "But what of the boy who dreamed of glory?"

"He met men who went to war." He looked at her. "My father used to visit the military hospitals, and he brought me along. I grew up listening to their stories. After my father died, I went in his stead. It's something I do to honor him and the men who fight for England."

She sobered. "So that is why you are working so hard for your resolution."

"Don't you see them?" he asked. "They're in every corner of London. The maimed, the hungry, the angry. If we are to avoid the fate of the French king, then we must take care of our people. Surely you see it, too."

She touched his arm, and he felt his muscles flex in reaction before relaxing beneath her heat. "I see it," she said. "And it does you credit that you do as well. So many of your set do not."

He nodded, startled that he had spoken so passionately to her. As a rule, talk with ladies was of the weather and the latest play. "I beg your pardon. I find myself frustrated with politics of late. This is your first outing to Hyde Park at the fashionable hour. I should not darken it with my ill temper."

She snorted. "This is not my first visit. I have spent many afternoons strolling at the outskirts to watch the fashionable go by."

"What?" he asked. "Where?"

"I'll show you my favorite place when we pass it. As for your ill temper, I find it interesting. It is not about losing money on a horse or a roll of the dice. It is not about how your first mistress is angry with your second or that your wife is spending your money faster than you can gamble it away."

"You must find better company," he groused.

"That is the whole purpose of this ride, is it not? To find me better company to marry?"

Well, that soured his temper even more, but he had to admit that he wanted her to find a better life than endless nights at the Lyon's Den. That wasn't much of a future for anyone, much less a fascinating woman.

"Tell me of your proposed law, my lord. Does it prosper? Will the resolution pass, do you think?"

"No," he muttered, thoroughly downcast. "I lost a vote yesterday. One that carries others, and I cannot see how to regain it."

"Oh, dear," she said. "Who defected?"

"Baron Easterly. He's in a monstrous foul mood, and he never agrees to anything when he's like that. I swear, he votes nay merely because he is angry with the world, and I cannot fathom what has happened or how to turn it around."

She chuckled. "His wife found out how much he spends at the brothels and has locked him out of her bedchamber in fury."

"What?"

She frowned at him. "Baron Easterly, right? He's the fat one with the bushy mustache. The one who frequents all the ladies just so they will crow about his prowess."

This was not a proper discussion to have with a lady, but he needed the information too much to worry about the niceties. "Yes, that's him. And his...appetites are rather legendary."

"They are indeed," she said with a grin, her eyes dancing in the sunlight. She was begging him to ask, daring him to continue with this topic, and he could not resist her when she looked so delighted.

"What do you know?"

"He has not touched a woman other than his wife in decades."

He blew out a breath. It was sweet that she was this naive. Sweet and a little disappointing. "Of course," he said placatingly. All men visited the brothels so that they could go home and make love to their wives.

"Listen!" she said. "He pays the women to tell his cronies how good he is. Then he sits in the chair and reads. Sometimes he talks about hunting with his dogs. We have had regular updates on how his son fares. The boy gets ill in the fall, but it always clears up by Michaelmas."

Could it be true? Interesting gossip to be sure, but he didn't know how to use it to his advantage. He would never threaten to expose the man for something so silly. If Easterly wanted to pay women to make him legendary, it was no business of Elliott's. Or anyone else's for that matter.

"The thing is," she continued, "it would be so much better for him to pick a single mistress, someone thought to be unattainable. He could pay her a pittance of what he spends all over town and still have the same illusion of prowess. More, in fact, if it could be arranged."

"That is not generally how mistresses work."

"And that is not generally how the upstairs ladies work. But it could be arranged, and then he could pay court to his wife, still appear manly before his cronies, and have a great deal more money with which to pamper his family. It would work all the way around and likely put him in an excellent mood."

Elliott wanted to argue. He wanted to claim that no man would spend his blunt on a mistress without taking advantage of what was offered. But he knew Baron Easterly. The man was short, fat, and balding. He took great pride in his reputation with women, and it wasn't impossible that he had spent a great deal to maintain an illusion.

"But could it be done?" he wondered. "What unattainable woman would agree to such a bargain?"

"The Abacas Woman," Amber said. "She's mysterious, gentlemen have been vying for her attention since she came to the Lyon's Den, and no man has claimed her."

The woman who sat in a cage with Amber and her grandfather? The one who was responsible for the money that flowed through the den. "Would she do it?"

Amber smiled. "What woman wouldn't? It is easy money."

Her reputation would be destroyed, but what reputation was that? No one knew who the Abacas Woman was. And for Easterly to land her would boost his reputation to legendary status.

Meanwhile, Amber cast him a coy look. "I should think Lord Easterly would be very grateful to the man who arranged that for him. Perhaps enough to vote his way on a resolution to aid veterans."

"He would indeed," Elliott breathed. "As I would be grateful to the woman who helped me arrange such a thing."

Amber grinned. "Would it be enough, then?"

"Enough what?"

She gestured ahead to the edge of the fashionable throng. "Enough to repay you for taking me here today? To sponsoring me tomorrow night at Almack's?" She looked at him, and when he didn't answer, she blew out a breath. "I am trying to be of service to you, my lord. To pay you back for the trouble of introducing me to the *ton*."

Of course, she was. Of course, she was *bartering* for his time with her. Because that is what people in her world did. They paid her for her time and her jewelry. "Does no one do things for you merely because they wish to help you?"

She stared at him in surprise, but he would not be deterred.

"Do all *men* of your acquaintance require recompense for your time?" As if she were no better than an upstairs lady, as she called them?

"I..." She began. "I thought..." But what she thought was not clear, at least not in her words. Elliott had no trouble understanding.

"Let me explain," he said firmly. "I am pleased to introduce you to the *ton*," he said, and it wasn't a lie. She was a delight, and he thought all worthy people would enjoy her company. "I am *honored* to escort you this afternoon and tomorrow night. I do not require payment nor barter from you. It is what a gentleman would do for a..." He was about to say a *gently reared lady*, but of course, she was nothing of the sort. "For you," he finally said. "Any gentlemen would be happy to sponsor you into his set."

She sighed. "I think we both know that is not true."

That he wasn't a gentleman? He wasn't, given what he'd tried to do with her last night. But he knew what she meant. Most of his set would disdain her simply because of her birth. "Well," he finally said, "perhaps my sister and I are cut from the same cloth. I do not find you in the least bit objectionable."

"Not objectionable," she drawled. "Damned by faint praise."

He blew out a breath. "Worthy, Miss Gohar. I find you worthy." And wasn't that a surprise? He wasn't one who thought the lower classes should be suppressed. He certainly wasn't one to bargain harshly one minute, then sneer at the crassness of it all in the next breath. But she was generally considered beneath him. And yet, he found her more engaging, more irresistible, and generally more *worthy* of his attention the more time he spent with her.

Which made it all the harder for him to turn his attention outward to the fashionable throng to acknowledge all the greedy gentlemen who came looking for an introduction. But that is exactly what a ride in Hyde Park was about, and that was quite explicitly what he had promised to do.

So, he did. He smiled and made her known to every eligible bachelor who had come to London this season looking for a wife. He kept his smile in place while she greeted them with the kind of composure absent in schoolroom misses and sheltered ladies. And he watched with growing anger as one gentleman after another was charmed by her.

She was his companion, she was his find, and she was absolutely, one hundred percent not for them! And yet, within the space of an hour, three gentlemen found a moment to ask if applications for her hand in marriage should go to Elliott or if there was a different relation at hand.

They weren't declarations, of course. There was a great deal of business to investigate before a proposal was in the offering. But the process had begun, and with his family's sponsorship, Amber could very well find herself choosing between suitors by week's end.

It was enough to make him invent an excuse to cut the ride short. But he could not do that to her. Anyone could see that she was enjoying herself immensely. This was the dream of a lifetime for a girl like her. And so, he bit back his growl and made yet another introduction. And they stayed there until the last eligible bachelor left.

CHAPTER TWELVE

AMBER NEVER IMAGINED that Almack's would be so boring. She'd been to one party. *One!* And already, she was tired of discussing the weather, fashion, and the latest play. No one wished to discuss politics or a secret passion. And the men seemed to think she would be fascinated by effusive compliments of her hair, her eyes, and even her teeth.

She enjoyed the dancing. And she especially loved being in a gown of palest blue, just like she'd imagined that night before all this began. She wasn't dripping with sapphires, but she did wear the gold lion in her hair. After a few minutes, even that grew boring. She missed her sketchbook, her family, and most especially, she missed working metal into a piece of art. She had seen more ugly jewelry in the last few days to make her itch to design something beautiful.

She wasn't complaining. Heavens knew this had been her dream since she had first heard of pretty dresses. She just hadn't expected reality to disillusion her so soon. There were only a few moments when her dreams felt as if they were as wonderful as she'd imagined, and those seconds were fast ticking away. It was when *he* danced with her, when *he* smiled at her, and when *he* said she was lovely, that she felt happy.

Elliott Rees, Lord Byrn. The man who had stayed away all day and offered no explanation of his absence when he came to fetch them for Almack's. The man who owed her nothing, and yet she was peeved when he didn't dance with her but once and anxious until he looked at her again. She was being illogical. He couldn't look at her while he was dancing with every girl in this wretched place. And he couldn't talk to her while he was saying pretty things to all those other richer, titled, or more beautiful girls.

"Thank you for the dance," Amber said to a gentleman with buck teeth and watery eyes. In truth, he was one of her better dance partners. He moved beautifully and spoke of something other than the weather, and it wasn't even about his dogs. He asked about Berlin and her life there, which, of course, was complete fabrication. She'd been grateful that the movements of the dance prevented her from anything but the most generic responses. She knew what to say, of course. She'd developed an elaborate past in the last few days, pulled from her very rich imagination. But it turned out that lying about who she was also paled over time.

Daydreams, it turned out, were never meant to come true. And that made her more depressed than she had ever been in her entire life.

"Amber, you should have told me!" Diana said as soon as Mr. Buck Teeth retreated. "I could have seeded the field so much better if I'd known."

Amber frowned. She had no idea what that meant.

"Don't look like that. It causes wrinkles," Diana said as she pulled her to sit in a nearby bench. The orchestra was taking a break, thank heaven, and Amber was grateful to get off her aching feet. "I just heard it from Lady Waterford, who heard it from her son who heard it from… Oh, I don't know who. But it's the talk of the evening and the reason you haven't stopped dancing all night long."

"What is the reason?" she asked, her voice sharper than she intended.

"Your dowry! I had no idea that you had one, much less twenty thousand pounds! That's enough to overcome your lack of a title. In fact, it's enough for you to be much more discerning as to your dance partners."

Twenty thousand pounds? But that was ridiculous. "I don't have a dowry," she said. And even if she did, it certainly wasn't any twenty thousand pounds. The amount was exorbitant!

"Actually, you do," said the one voice she'd been straining to hear all day. Elliott stood beside them, holding out two glasses of lemonade. "I spoke with your father this afternoon. He seemed honored to bestow a dowry upon his only child. In fact, that was his exact word, honored."

Amber stared opened mouthed at the man. She saw his blank expression and his long fingers where they held her glass. She saw his black attire and a stickpin for his cravat shaped like a flame. It was the pin that jarred her out of her shock, for it was one she had fashioned herself.

"I made that pin," she said stupidly. "Did you buy it today?" It was a ridiculous thing to focus on, but he was wearing something of hers. Something she had fashioned with her own hand, and for some reason, that stood out as significant to her.

"Actually, your father gifted it to me. When we spoke about your marriage."

"My marriage?" she echoed dumbly. Then her heart abruptly beat triple time in her throat. "You spoke to my father about marrying me?" He words came out as a kind of squeak.

His eyes widened in surprise, and he swallowed convulsively. "Well, um, as to that—"

"You don't want him," Diana inserted before he could finish. "He's only interested in politics. But as soon as we are home, I shall make a list of the best gentlemen to consider." She was about to prattle on further, but Elliott interrupted.

"I have had a couple men ask me about your particulars after our ride in Hyde Park. I spoke with your father, and he has given me leave to assist him with this task."

The blood was still rushing through her ears and throbbing in her temples. "My marriage is a task?" she asked, her tongue as thick as her muddled thoughts.

Diana patted her hand. "Your dowry is. The marriage contract." She squeezed Amber's fingers. "I am thrilled that we can be true friends now. You can marry a respectable man, and we can visit one other every day if we like." The excitement in her voice was palpable.

"We weren't friends before?" Good lord, she was being completely muttonheaded. Of course, they weren't real friends. The difference in their station precluded that. But if she married well, then Lady Dunnamore and Mrs. Whomever She Became could become dear friends without a word of censure from anyone.

"Twenty thousand pounds," Diana breathed. "I had no idea."

Neither had Amber. And the idea made her sick to her stomach. It felt like she had been branded with a pound note and then set in the stocks to sell as a prize cow. Until this moment, this had been a holiday from the cage. A time to dance and wear pretty dresses, knowing for certain that at the end of it all, she would return to her home, her family, and her friends. And yes, the damned gray cage. But that was all part of the package of her life.

And now she was to be sold off in marriage? Certainly, she knew about marriage contracts, but she never thought that she would have one. Never thought that her father would negotiate for the best value in a husband as he would a lot of uncut stones.

She abruptly stood up, nearly spilling the lemonade that Lord Byrn still held in his hand. "I need to talk to my father," she said tightly. She needed to know where he had found twenty thousand pounds. And why he wanted to be rid of her so desperately. Who would sit in the cage with her grandfather? Who would fashion jewelry for the store? Who would see that there were coals in the grate in winter and heavy blankets to keep them warm?

Those were things she did for her family. She had always done them since before her mother passed. And now they didn't want her anymore? It couldn't be. And yet the pain in her chest told her it was true.

"Miss Gohar. Miss—Amber! Wait!"

She jolted to a stop, only now realizing that she was halfway to the door. Everyone around them was staring at her as Lord Byrn made it to her side. "This isn't seemly," he said under his breath.

Seemly? It wasn't at all seemly to sell a daughter like livestock. Meanwhile, Diana made it to her side. She spoke loud enough for all to overhear.

"Don't worry, my dear. Your grandmother will be just fine. I'm sure it's nothing serious, but we can go home and send a letter right away. There is no reason to worry."

Her grandmother had died before she was born, but she recognized it for the ruse that it was. Diana had to give some excuse for her sudden distress, and that was as good as anything.

"I'll get your wraps," Lord Byrn said. Then he looked her in the eyes. "Don't be concerned. I'll take care of everything."

That was exactly the problem! He had taken care of talking with her father and getting her a dowry. Diana was taking care of finding her a husband. And no one was taking care of what she wanted at all.

But the moment she thought it, she knew it for the lie it was. Hadn't all of this been exactly what she'd prayed for? The parties, the dancing, the *husband* to whisk her away to a life of ease. She had dreamed of exactly that, and suddenly it was possible. With twenty thousand pounds, she might even garner a husband with a title. And though that was still not likely, it wasn't out of reach anymore. Suddenly, she didn't like reaching at all. She just wanted to be home, where no one complimented her teeth or spoke about their dogs. Where she was nothing and no one at all but the girl who daydreamed and made jewelry in secret.

And now, damn it, she was about to cry. What was wrong with her?

"Here you go," Lord Byrn said as he set her wrap upon her shoulders. Then he gave her his right arm and his sister his left before escorting them outside to his waiting carriage.

"Really, Amber," Diana began, "this is something to celebrate."

Was it?

"It's just new," Elliott said. "And new is always frightening."

Is that what they thought? Of course, it was. Because to them, the buying and selling of wives was how things were done. Except it had never been done that way for her. Everyone had assumed that eventually, she would meet someone and fall in love. A butcher's boy or a baker's son. No one but her had dreamed of a prince at a ball.

She didn't speak as they climbed into the carriage. The coachman started them moving, but she just stared at her hands. She wore fine kid gloves borrowed from Diana. Would she one day have fine things like this of her own? Provided by a wealthy, titled husband? She had good things, of course. Her family wasn't rich, but they'd always had coal in the winter and sturdy gloves for her hands. But now she might have fine gloves and gowns with lace made in France.

The idea made her head swim.

"I'll take her to see her father," Elliott said to Diana. "But she can't be seen like this."

"No, of course not. I have a dark cloak at home. I'll bring it out to you."

"Thank you."

Diana leaned close and squeezed Amber's fingers. "You look like I did before my wedding. But it won't be like that for you," she said. "You get to pick your husband, and I can help," she said. "I know a little of who might make a good husband and who would not."

So did Amber. She saw the ones for the *not* column every night. In fact, that was the first requirement of any possible husband, that he not frequent the Lyon's Den. "I don't understand," she finally said. "We don't have twenty thousand pounds." Why would her father promise something they didn't have?

"Actually," Lord Byrn said gently, "you do. It was my suggestion. You have that much in gemstones and future profits from the store. Many gentlemen will marry a woman in the trades for just that kind of future income. The connection is usually kept quiet, but it is not uncommon."

It was his suggestion. How the idea hurt. She couldn't even fully say why, but the thought of him suggesting ways to make her more *auctionable* was a betrayal that burned deep in her heart.

"My grandparents married for love. They were both poor, but he was apprenticed to a jeweler, and she could cook. They had dreams together and made them come true. He tells me the stories often."

Diana patted her hand. "And now you will have a marriage based on something much more substantial than dreams."

She had no response to that, so she kept her head bowed, her fingers clasped, and her mouth pressed tightly shut. Her mind was spinning, and her emotions were even worse. She remained like that as they stopped at Diana's home. His sister left, only to return with a cloak and to press a kiss to Amber's cold cheek.

"I can't go with you to the Den. It would be disastrous if anyone saw me, but Elliott will keep you safe."

Amber looked up in confusion. "There is no one there who will hurt me."

"Of course not," Elliott said as he wrapped the dark fabric around her. "But this is about your reputation. Leave the hood over your head so no one will recognize you."

No one would recognize her at her own home? Because she had a cloak with a hood on? She knew he meant it the other way. None of the fashionable people at the Lyon's Den would see her, but she couldn't help but hear it the other way. If she married someone outside her set, someone titled and respectable, would she then forever have to visit her family in secret? With her head and face covered so no one would know?

"I am being ridiculous," she said, her voice disgustingly weak. "Every girl wants this. I want this." So, why was she rushing home to plead with her father to take it all back? "I am the luckiest girl alive."

He didn't argue, but he also didn't agree. Instead, he pulled her hand into his. They sat together like that, hand in hand, as the carriage drove through the London streets. Bit by bit, the neighborhood grew darker and more dangerous. The smell of sewage grew stronger, and she knew the rookeries were close.

This was not something she would miss. She was accustomed to the danger, only going out during the day and in clothing that attracted no attention. And even then, she was often accompanied by one of the Wolf Pack.

If she were to ride in a fine carriage, though, would she be in more danger or less? Would she need to hire footmen who could protect her, or would her family have to come see her in a different part of town?

Thank heavens, they arrived quickly at the Lyon's Den because she kept thinking of more questions, more problems, and more details that had never occurred in her daydreams. There, everything was perfectly easy, but suddenly the details were too much to bear. As soon as the horses stopped, she pushed open the door.

"Amber!" Elliott called, but she was too quick, and she knew this place well. She heard him following her. His heavy tread was close behind as she dashed around the corner of the building to the small door in the back of the shop.

It was locked. It was after dark. So, she banged on it, crying out as she hammered on the door.

"Papa! Open up! Papa!"

No one answered, and her cries grew more frantic until she was sobbing at the door. Lord Byrn joined her and gently pulled her fists from the door. "Think Amber. Where would your father usually be right now?"

"In the back, cutting stones!"

"But then who would be with your grandfather?"

"I would." Except she had been at Almack's. She took a breath and tried to think. "They're both upstairs," she said quietly. She turned and headed for the ladies' entrance, only to realize that Lord Byrn would not be able to join her that way. It was not a problem. After all, she'd spent nearly her entire life going in and out of the Den without his company. But at this moment, he was the only touchstone she had in a world gone crazy. She didn't want to leave his side.

"We can go in the main entrance," she said softly. "Women sometimes enter that way."

He didn't question her. He simply extended his forearm to her. She didn't want to take it. She wanted to hold his hand like they had in the carriage, but this was better than nothing. She would hold onto his arm and feel his solid presence that way. She set her palm to his arm, and he covered it with his free hand while tucking her close to his side.

"I do not understand what you are feeling right now, but I will not leave your side until you are comfortable. Agreed?"

"Yes," she exhaled, relief in the word. "Thank you."

They made it inside with little issue. Lord Byrn was welcome here, as well as any of his companions, even if she be female and entering through the wrong door. Amber ran up the steps as soon as they made it inside and headed straight to the cage. But as soon as she got to the main floor, the noise and the smell assaulted her. Smoke, stale spirits, and sweat made for a nauseating atmosphere. She coughed just as a burst of raucous laughter filled the room. This was so familiar to her, like a second skin, and yet it didn't seem to fit her now. Compared to the pastel colors and sedate dancing of Almack's, this was a decidedly male environment, and not a very nice one.

Nevertheless, she rushed forward, going straight to the cage door. "Papa!" she whispered through the grate. "Papa, open up. It's me."

The door immediately opened, but not by her father. It was Lina, the Abacas Woman. "Thisbe!" she cried. "What are you doing here?"

Thisbe. The name she used at the den, jolting her yet again. She'd gotten used to being called Amber and Miss Gohar. "Where is my father?"

"He's gone to get some tea for your grandfather. Come in, come in."

She opened the cage door and pulled Amber inside. Lord Byrn was right behind her, and if Lina tried to block him out, she was unsuccessful.

"*Enkelin?* Is that you?" It was her grandfather using the German name for granddaughter, and she rushed to the back of the tiny room to hug him. Unlike the other smells, his scent was welcome and reassuring.

"I'm here now, Grandfather."

"But why? Aren't you to be a fine lady now?"

The very words brought tears to her eyes, and she couldn't answer. Meanwhile, Lina took her hand and pressed her forehead to it in a kind of bow. Few knew that Lina was from China, and this was her way of giving respect.

"Thank you, Thisbe," Lina said. "Thank you."

"What?"

"Thank you for helping me get the money I need to send for my sister in China. Thank you for sending Lord Easterly to me."

What? "But—"

"I took your suggestion," Lord Byrn said, his voice a low rumble by her ear. "The arrangement was made this afternoon, as you recommended."

It had? She looked at Lord Byrn. "You accomplished all that this afternoon?"

"As you said yesterday, it was a beneficial plan for everyone." Elliott's smile flashed white in the gloom. "And Lord Easterly vows to support my resolution and bring his friends' votes along with him."

Oh, good. That was good news.

"I need only to secure Lord Morthan's vote with the brooch, then everything will be in hand. And you will be well on your way to being married respectably. You need never return to this cage again." His opinion of the tiny dark cage was abundantly clear. And now that she stood in it, she noticed how very small it was, how it smelled as bad as the main floor, if not worse. Now that she looked about, she realized that it was a fraction of the size of the bedroom she had at Lady Dunnamore's home.

How had she spent so much time here?

And now it became even more cramped as her father came in.

Lina retreated back to her corner, lifting her abacas and beginning the steady click-clack of her work. Lord Byrn backed into the other corner, clearly trying to be as small as possible, which was hard given the breadth of his shoulders and his height. Her father set down the tea before her grandfather, then turned to her with a big smile.

"Have you come to thank me, my girl?" he said with a hearty laugh. "You always said you would marry a prince, and look at you now. My grandsons will go to English schools with titled lords, and you will teach them to never come to a place like this, yes?"

What was she to say to that? The idea that her sons would never know this place was wonderful, but that was like saying they would never know their own mother.

"Papa, why didn't you tell me?"

"Tell you what? Things I never dreamed possible? It was Lord Byrn who arranged it. You must do a good piece for him. The best you can make, for he has been generous with you. A good bargain, yes? You make a brooch and get a fine husband in return."

Was that how he saw it? A brooch for a husband, as if the two were marketable commodities.

"It is too cramped in here," her father said. "We will go downstairs."

Amber jolted in surprise. Her father never invited gentlemen to go down to the shop unless he intended to sell them something. "But what if someone comes to the cage?" Her grandfather hadn't been able to accurately appraise anything for at least a year.

"Lina will send word, yes?"

Lina nodded in agreement.

"See? All good." Then he turned to Lord Byrn. "We did not have time this afternoon for a toast. Let us go share a drink now, yes?"

"It would be my pleasure, Mr. Gohar."

Her father snorted. "I left that name a long time ago. I am Mr. Gold here."

He was Mr. Gold. She was Amber Gohar. And everybody wanted her to become Mrs. Somebody Else. Everybody, that is, except her. But no one was asking her. So, when Elliott and her father went downstairs, she followed like a silly child and said absolutely nothing.

CHAPTER THIRTEEN

ELLIOTT FOLLOWED MR. Gold down the steps to the jewelry shop below. He smiled and nodded, making comments when needed, but his attention was centered on Amber as she trailed along behind them. She was withdrawn, her eyes haunted, and her hands clasped in front of her. Which was completely opposite of the woman he had come to know. She was unusually direct for a woman, she always held her head high, and her hands were often the most animated part of her. But not right now, and he was struggling to figure out why. If she were his mother, he'd just say she was in a mood, but Amber was the most unflappable woman he'd ever met. Until today.

And all because her father had given her a dowry?

"I cut some new stones today," her father said as he opened the door to the back of the shop. "Why don't you see what design you can fashion for them?"

Obviously, he was talking to Amber, who looked up at her father first, then over to Elliott. "I do not like it when you discuss my future without me." Her voice was firm and yet still respectful.

"Then leave the door open. You can hear everything we say. But if I am to lose my best designer, then I must have a few more things to sell before she goes."

Amber sighed. "I am your only designer."

"Not anymore," her father returned. "I have a new apprentice. He draws beautifully, and he began today."

Elliott saw Amber jerk in reaction. "Papa—" she began, her voice breaking.

"You were always going to grow up, *Juwel*," he said softly, using the German word for jewel. "But even so, you will always be my daughter, and whenever you wish to sculpt, you can come here."

She said nothing, but a sheen of tears was in her eyes. Her father hugged her, and she clasped him with a grip hard enough to turn her knuckles white. It was an intimate scene, and Elliott felt his chest tighten as he watched father and daughter say good-bye. They weren't, of course. Amber would always be welcome here, and her father would always adore her. And yet, that was the way the moment felt. As if Amber were about to leave forever.

They stood there hugging for a long, long time until Amber lowered her arms. Her cheeks were wet, and she ducked her head away from Elliott. "I'll go see what this new apprentice has done," she said gruffly.

Her father snorted. "Nothing good, but there is talent there."

She nodded and went into a room deep inside the building. She turned up lamps until the room was as bright as daylight, and Elliott looked in to see a workroom with a place for cutting stones, another with pencils and paper, plus carving knives and wax, and then an entire corner given to a kiln.

"This is where I cut stones, and she designs the jewelry," her father said proudly. "When she was a child, she would spend every extra moment in here watching me and her grandfather work. She sketched until she could carve. I had meant for her to work the front of the shop because a pretty girl always helps with sales, but her genius is here. With the wax."

Elliott had never seen jewelry made before. He'd never even thought to ask, and so he listened with interest as her father explained. "She carves the wax and makes something like this." He held up a ring sculpted in wax. There was a place for the stone, raised leaves to twine around it, and a thick band, all exquisitely detailed. "This is put in here," he held up a metal flask, "and we surround it with a special plaster, then wait until it hardens. Then we put it in the kiln, and the wax melts away."

"Leaving behind a mold," Elliott said as he looked at an entire shelf of molds for rings, pendants, and brooches.

"She designed all of those," Mr. Gold said, pointing at the top shelf. "A true artist, my daughter. Her hands were made for this work."

Amber shot her father a wry look, and Elliott immediately guessed her thoughts. She was wondering—if her hands were made for this work—why had he dowered her so well as to marry away from it? This kind of work wouldn't be acceptable in a titled lady. It was considered a trade, for all that she seemed a true artist at it.

"Come, come," Mr. Gold said as he tugged on Elliott's sleeve. "Leave her to criticize the new boy's sketches. We will drink and discuss matters."

He wasn't sure what there was to discuss, but this was Mr. Gold's show, and so, he followed silently into the main showroom.

"We live upstairs," Mr. Gold said. "Top floor where there is better sun. But that is not fit for company. So, we sit here near my treasure, and we drink to her health." From his expression, it was clear he meant his daughter was his treasure, not the gemstones or jewelry contained in this place.

"I will drink to that," Elliott said.

Mr. Gold brought out a small table and chairs and set them in the center of the showroom. Then he produced a brandy fine enough that Elliott's brows rose in surprise.

"When I toast my daughter, we drink the best," Mr. Gold said.

Such pride in his voice, such love in his every word and gesture. Elliott couldn't stop a pang of envy. His own father had passed before he'd seen Elliott grown. Worse, Elliott had been at school when the man was ill and had never had a chance to say goodbye. If his father had lived, would he beam with pride like Mr. Gold did? Would he pull out the finest brandy and drink to Elliott's future?

He would never know. But in the absence of his own father, he would make merry with Amber's. He toasted to her health, to her future, to a husband who understood how to make her happy.

"And how would he do that?" Elliott asked, his body warm with drink and good cheer.

"I tell you," Mr. Gold said as he leaned forward. "When we left Germany, my baby girl cried. She cried and cried because she had cousins, you see. Family we have never seen again. I tried everything to make her happy. I plied her with sweets, sang to her at night, even carried her around like a baby when she had nightmares, and she was no baby then. It was heavy to carry an eight-year-old all night."

Elliott laughed. "I'm sure it was."

"And do you know what her mother said to me when my arms were aching and my throat so dry from singing? She told me to leave the child alone. Amber will always find her way in her own way. She is like her mother in that. Her mother did things as she chose, and woe to any man to tell her different." Admiration rang in his tone.

"And did Amber find her way?"

"She did. She picked up my carving knife and made a bird of wax so she could fly back home whenever she wanted."

"Really? Do you have it?"

He snorted. "No! It was a badly done. What eight-year-old can carve a bird? But she had stopped crying, and so I let her keep carving." He threw back the rest of his drink, then stretched out his legs with a smile. "I trust you, my lord, with my greatest treasure. Find her a husband who will let her find her own way, yes?"

Elliott fidgeted with his drink. There were plenty of disinterested husbands in the *ton*. Indeed, most couldn't care less about their wives beyond the getting of an heir, but he had never thought that a recipe for a happy marriage. He glanced behind him. He could see Amber through the door as she wielded a small knife with deft fingers. He could not see what she made, but he could see the absolute concentration on her face.

"You want her to be able to keep carving for you," he said quietly. No doubt, her designs brought in a great deal of money.

"Not for me," the man said with a frown. "Most buyers have no imagination. A ring with diamonds around it. Bah. Boring. Even the new apprentice will do that within a year. No, her carving is for her, and her husband must let her do it." He flicked his glance back into the room where Amber seemed completely absorbed in her work. "See? No tears."

"But I still have ears," Amber said loudly, though her gaze never wavered from what she made in her hands. "And I will select my husband, not Lord Byrn."

"Of course, of course," her father said with a fond smile. Then he spoke softly, in an undertone that only Elliott could hear. "But you will see that she selects from only the best, yes?"

"She has a level head and has seen the men in the Den. I doubt she will choose someone ruinous."

Mr. Gold shot him with a stern look. It said without words that her father expected him to make sure that Amber chose wisely. Elliott nodded his agreement. Nothing was said aloud, but the bargain was struck.

They relaxed back in their chairs, then, and spoke of gentlemanly things. Her father had an interest in politics, and their discussion was heated at times, but no less invigorating. Mr. Gold brought a continental perspective to the matters in England, and the evening passed with exceptional good cheer. Until the man stretched and yawned.

"It is late, and my eyes are blurry. You will see my daughter returned safely to Lady Dunnamore's? She will likely want to carve for several more hours."

Really? It was almost midnight.

Mr. Gold shrugged when he saw Elliott look at his pocket watch. "A true artist never considers the time." It was clear that Amber was indeed a true artist. "And in case you worry for your safety, the doors are well locked, and Amber is very good with knives."

That was Mr. Gold's way of reminding Elliott to behave around his daughter, and that Amber would likely stab him if he tried anything unseemly.

"I have no doubt that she could gut me, if she chose to."

Mr. Gold flashed him a drunken grin but didn't speak. Amber spoke instead.

"There is no need for him to stay, Papa. I will sleep upstairs tonight."

"You will not," Mr. Gold said sternly. "A true lady does not spend her nights here." He made an expansive gesture at the Den and the surrounding neighborhood. "Besides, the boy sleeps with us now. There is no room for a fine lady like you."

Amber lifted her gaze to her father, and her eyes again held the sheen of tears. "I am not a fine lady yet."

Her father laughed. "Little *Juwel*, you have been a fine lady since you could put on a pretty dress and dance the Landler." He looked to Elliott. "She learned the steps when she was six. That is when she first told me she would marry a prince." He crossed slowly into the workroom to press a sloppy kiss to her forehead. She returned it in a much neater fashion, and then together, they inspected her carving.

It was a firebird, wings upstretched with flame at its feet. The feathers were precise, the flames exquisite, and the whole creation entirely lifelike. It took Elliott's breath away.

"Very good," her father said with a grunt. "What stone for the eye?"

"A ruby. Not too large—"

"But of excellent quality. Yes. I have just the stone." He turned to a wooden case with narrow drawers, but his gestures were too large and too imprecise. Amber had to hunch over the wax to protect it.

"Papa! Be careful."

He righted himself quickly. "I think I shall head to bed and look at the stones tomorrow."

"An excellent idea," Amber returned.

"And you will go back to Lady Dunnamore's with Lord Byrn." He waggled his eyebrows. "Stab him if he is not the gentleman I think he is."

"Papa!" Amber cried, her cheeks coloring. "A fine father you are, leaving me alone and telling me to defend my own honor."

Mr. Gold's expression tightened. "Do I need to stay?"

She sighed and shook her head. "No, Papa. Lord Byrn is a perfect gentleman."

That was decidedly untrue, but Elliott knew better than to say a word. Instead, he gave the man his most respectful bow. "I will take care of her, Mr. Gohar. Have no fear."

Her father nodded. "And if you don't, the Wolf Pack sits right there." He pointed to the back door and the stairs that led up to the den.

He was talking about the bouncers who would come running in mass if Amber raised her voice in any way. "I believe you are protected better than most princesses," he said dryly.

She shrugged, and Mr. Gold grinned. "You understand us." Then with a broad wave, he opened that very same back door only to stop short at the sight of a small boy with dark curly hair asleep on the floor. His head was lolling against the thick leg of a very large-fisted man seated there. And though one of his hands had gone lax over a piece of foolscap, the other still clutched a thin piece of charcoal.

"The new apprentice?" Amber asked, her voice dry.

Her father grunted as he gingerly tugged the foolscap out of the boy's hand to study the image there. A soldier and his horse, neither one very good, but both with a bold stroke that spoke of spirit if not skill.

"He thinks the ladies will wear brooches of soldiers," Mr. Gold said as he showed the drawing to Amber.

"His heart is with the horse."

"Isn't every boy's? Especially when they grow up in the rookeries with nothing to see but dirty stone, rotting wood, and rats."

Amber pulled the foolscap from her father's hand, her eyes narrowing as she studied it. She was silent a long time before she handed it back. "He is better than I was at that age."

"With the horse, yes."

"And the soldier."

"But not the birds. You always looked to the sky." Her father pressed another kiss to Amber's forehead. "You, daughter, will fly far. This one, however, will stay on the land, I think. He is good with dogs, too."

"What's his name?"

"Joseph."

Amber stepped forward and then gently shook the child awake. Elliott watched her closely to see if she would be mean to the boy who would likely take her place in the family business. He shouldn't have worried. Her touch was gentle, her voice soft.

"Joseph. Wake up, Joseph."

The boy opened his eyes with the sudden alertness of a child who had seen too much danger. He jerked away from Amber, and his eyes darted about, but he never let go of the charcoal.

"Hello, Joseph," Amber said quietly. "Do you know who I am?"

The boy nodded but didn't speak.

"It is late, young man. You should be in bed."

The child knuckled his eyes, leaving a dark charcoal smear across his face. "I was waiting."

"For me?" Mr. Gold asked. "Did you want something?"

The boy shook his head, and that was all the answer he needed to say. Everyone could see he just wanted to be with safe people and keep an eye on the man who was providing for him.

Joseph scrambled to his feet. "I can help you go upstairs now. If you need it."

"I do need it," Mr. Gold said. It was a lie. The man had certainly made merry with his drink, but he would have made it to the top floor without incident. "I thank you, young Joseph. Come, let us get your face cleaned before sleep." Mr. Gold used his thumb to try and wipe away the charcoal smear.

Joseph wrinkled his nose and ducked his head away, but he allowed Mr. Gold to clean him a little. And the whole time, he watched Amber with a steady gaze. "Have you come to take your bed back?"

"No, Joseph. You may sleep there with no fear. I will never take your place away."

The relief was apparent in the child's entire body. He tried to cover it, but his shoulders eased down, he stood taller beside Mr. Gold, and eventually, his lips curved into a shy smile. "One day, I will carve you a big soldier with a large hat and a sharp sword. He will be the most handsome soldier you have ever seen."

"I would rather see a horse from you. Or maybe a dog."

A grin filled his whole face. "I will make both."

"I believe you will." Then she smiled. "Go on now. Get Papa to bed."

So, it was done. Both boy and father climbed the stairs, leaving behind the large man in the chair smiling at her with a toothy grin.

"How are you doing, Philostrate?" Amber asked when her father and Joseph were out of sight.

The man made a happy gurgling sound as his grin widened.

"I'm so glad." Then she squeezed the man's massive arm. "I won't be much longer." She glanced at Elliott. "He always waits there when I work late."

Elliott gave the man a brief nod. "Sir."

"He doesn't speak. We don't know why, but he never has. And he is the best guardian a princess could ever want."

Philostrate gave her a fond smile, waited for her and Elliott to step back into the jewelry shop, then he shut the door to give her the illusion of privacy, but not before giving Elliott a long threatening glare. For a girl deemed not respectable by most of society, she certainly had a great many protectors.

And so they were alone. Or at least somewhat private.

"That was kind of you," he said. "Letting Joseph feel safe here."

"Really?" Amber asked. "I only told him the truth. He will always have a place here now that Papa has adopted him."

"And what of your place?" he pressed. "Don't you feel cast aside?"

He knew she did. He could see it on her face and in the way she had looked at the boy's drawings. But in this, she surprised him. She exhaled a long, unhappy sigh.

"I had not expected to become grown in the space of two days. For years I have pushed my father to let me have more freedom. Always he has said no. And then you appear, and suddenly I am free to do as I choose, to marry where I will."

That wasn't exactly true. She wasn't fully free. She was under his protection. She had no money of her own, and no real independence could be had without it. And yet, she'd spent much of her life in a gray cage. What she had now must feel like stepping out unfettered into the world.

"So, why do you seem so sad?"

She looked at him and shrugged. Then she echoed his own words back to him. "It is only new. And new is often frightening."

"You will always be safe with me." He meant it. No matter where she went or who she married, he would always keep an eye out for her happiness. "May I see what you've made?" he asked as he gestured to her wax carving.

"Of course." She stepped away from the worktable as he approached, but there was little room in the tight space. He could feel the heat of her body and heard the tight, shallow way she breathed. Was she nervous about his opinion? She shouldn't be. The design was exquisite.

"Did you sketch this first?"

She shook her head. "No. I have been making that bird since I was a child. This is just the latest version." She leaned down to look closer at it. "But it is the first time that I have added flames." She slanted him a look. "I suppose you are to blame for that. Did you know that I made your stickpin?"

"Your father told me." He touched the flame pin in his cravat. "I underestimated you again, Miss Gohar. I thought this piece extraordinary, but I had no idea that you could do this," he said, gesturing to the bird in flight.

She looked down at it and then idly crushed it with one hand.

"What are you doing?" he gasped as he leaped forward to save the design. It was too late. The wax lay in pieces on the table. "Why?"

"It was too large to make into real jewelry. We do not have enough gold. Besides," she said with a shrug, "the head was too big and the throat too long."

He had not seen such flaws, but obviously, she had exacting standards. "I cannot believe you destroyed something that beautiful. You spent hours on that!"

"I cannot believe you sat with my father for hours. He has never done that with any man except my grandfather."

Elliott's smile was wistful. "I never got the chance to drink brandy with my own father. It was a pleasure to do so with yours."

She seemed to think about that, her expression grave. Then she lifted her chin. "I do not care what my father has said. You will not be the one to choose my husband."

He lifted his hands in surrender. "I shall merely advise you. I have every expectation that you will select an excellent husband. But if you are to be a respectable woman, I should get you home to my sister's immediately. We cannot risk you being seen here. Miss Amber Gohar and Thisbe Gold cannot be connected."

She looked around the cramped room. "And if I want to return here? To see my family or sculpt something new?"

He blew out a breath. "If you are careful, I can arrange for it." After all, many of his sister's new footmen worked here. They could be trusted to bring her safely. Though that thought made his gut tighten. He did not like the idea of any man other than himself escorting her.

"Good," she said as she gathered the broken pieces of her carving and threw them into a bag half filled with broken wax. "Let me get my cloak, and we can go."

He was there before her, shaking out the fabric before draping it gently around her. She pulled it about her neck, but when she would have stepped away from him, he tightened his hold on her shoulders.

"Your father was right," he said softly. "You are an artist. You must find a husband who will allow you to do this work."

She turned slightly in his hold, lifting her face to his. "Do you think that likely?" she asked, hope in her voice. "Is there a man among the *ton* who would want his wife in trade?"

"Ladies paint, Amber. And stitch and—"

"Pour molten gold into a flask and fire it in a kiln?" She lifted her bare hands such that he could see every bump and ridge. "I have cut myself a thousand times and burned myself as well. Aren't ladies supposed to have hands as soft as down?"

Yes, they were. He caught her hand, feeling every scar and callous that marred her skin. "Pick a husband who knows your value beneath your skin." Then he pulled her hand up to his lips, pressing a kiss into her palm. If there were scars beneath his lips, he didn't feel them. He only knew her scent and the way her hand cupped his face.

She leaned against him, stroking his chin as he pressed his mouth to her hand. He felt his body tighten in reaction, and he struggled to keep himself from wrapping his arms around her. The worktable was right beside them. He could do so many things to her right here, right now. And she seemed willing, her body pliable as her fingertips stroked across his cheek.

He pulled back. "You tempt me," he accused softly.

"You confuse me."

He drew back. "How so?"

"My father believes you to be a gentleman. I do, as well."

She didn't sound like that was a compliment. "Thank you?"

"You have arranged for my dowry and mean to help me select a husband."

That was true, though the knowledge gave him no pleasure.

Her voice dropped to a whisper. "And yet, I think about what we did in the carriage, and I want it again." Her gaze caught his. "Will there be no more of that?"

"I was a cad," he said harshly. "You are not a woman to be handled so crudely. I am ashamed of my actions." But he didn't regret them.

She blew out a breath that skated across his chin. "I wanted what happened. I begged for it."

Of course, she had, because she was an innocent. He knew better. He knew that he had created the desire in her because he wanted to experience it. Because he wanted her. And now again, he knew he should step away, but instead, he breathed her scent, he stood close enough to feel her heat, and he allowed it to stoke the need in both of them.

"You will not kiss me again?" Her voice was so quiet as to be near silent. But he read the words off her lips. And he felt her desire like a sweet shiver that he could stroke into a great quake.

He lowered his head until his lips touched her ear. When he spoke, he kept his words as quiet as hers had been. "Can you feel and keep silent? You have a protector right beyond the door."

She nodded.

And now the more important question. "Can you let me kiss you and not dream of more between us? Nothing has changed for me. I cannot marry for love. To do so would give up all my hopes in politics. Only men with the right wives influence the Crown." He said the words by rote because he had been saying that to himself ever since that first night in the carriage with her.

He had such plans for the country, ideas he wanted to implement, things that would steer the nation away from disaster. But that only came with great money or the right connections. He did not have a nabob's wealth. Thanks to Lord Dunnamore's mismanagement, their money was barely adequate. That left him working constantly to recover their finances, all while looking for connections in the evening, discussing resolutions and laws with the influential lords as he paid respect to their daughters.

It was what he'd been doing at Almack's this night. Whenever he hadn't been looking at Amber, that is. And it was the litany he repeated to himself when he wanted to spread her thighs and watch her come apart in his arms again.

"I cannot have you," he said. "But I could show you more if you want it."

She shifted in his arms, but she did not pull away. Neither forward nor back, and the movement showed she was as undecided as he. "For a man who is ashamed, you sound very unrepentant."

He closed his eyes as he pressed his forehead to hers. He felt the throb in his body, and his hands tightened reflexively around her waist. How easy it would be to slide his hands upward to her breasts. How wonderful it would be to ease her backward onto the worktable and feast upon her body.

"I want you, Amber," he said honestly. "More than I have ever wanted any woman before. I watch you when you dance, I dream of you when I sleep, and when I lie in bed and close my eyes, I have done such things with you. Such beautiful, wonderful, lustful things."

He heard her breath catch and felt her body soften against him. She wanted him, too.

"You do not understand the weight I feel every day," he continued. "What I owe my name, my family, and my country. It is not a vague thing to me, Amber, but a responsibility bred into me with my first breath. It is a factor in everything I do. Sometimes I hate it, but other times…" His voice trailed away.

"Yes?" she pressed. "Other times what?"

He sighed. "Other times, it is an honor I bear proudly. My title means something to the people I serve, to my forebearers, and to my future children. Your father changed his name from Gohar to Gold, maybe not as easy as changing his coat, but he did it nonetheless."

He felt her shoulders stiffen, then release as she absorbed the words he spoke.

"I cannot do the same. To be a Byrn means—"

"That you cannot marry a Gohar or a Gold." She gently moved out of his arms. "But you can take your pleasure with one?"

He nodded. It was the way things were done. Mistresses were common, marriages were sacred, though not in the way the priests would have one believe. Marriages were holy connections of power and privilege. And as fascinating and talented as Amber was, she had neither.

"I won't be your mistress," she said firmly.

"I understand."

"I won't let you touch me like…"

"Like I did in the carriage."

For the third time this night, he saw tears glittering in her eyes.

Before they were meant for her father, but this time, they were for him and her. For what they might have been together if only things were different.

"But I want it," she whispered, her voice desperate. "I want to feel those things with you. Is that wrong?"

"Of course not. Because if it is, then we are both damned."

She turned away. "It's not fair," she murmured, and he agreed.

And then he had an idea. A scandalous, horrible idea, but one that might serve. At least for her.

"What if I teach you?" he offered.

She blinked as she looked up at him. "What?"

"What if I teach you how to feel that way without me? Without anyone. You can do it yourself in your own bed."

She frowned. "It cannot be the same."

It wasn't. It wasn't even close. "It might feel the same. You would have to try."

"How?"

He glanced at the door. This was not something to be done with a guard ten feet away. "I will tell you—"

"In the carriage?"

He felt his lips twist in a rueful smile. "The basics can be learned quickly. We need not take a long ride around Hyde Park."

She nodded slowly. "And if I want more than the basics?"

He shook his head, though the motion felt stiff with his muscles clenched tight. "I would be tempted too much."

"Very well," she said. "The basics."

He nearly took her then. He could pin her against the wall and devour her until she screamed with desire. His belly tightened, and his groin throbbed along with his pounding heart.

But he was a man of his word. And though he struggled with it, he was also a gentleman who would not betray her father or his own family name. He held back. He gestured for her to precede him out the door. And he waited until he could adequately hide his state before stepping with her along the street.

Eventually, they came to his carriage. He handed her in and sat beside her, feeling her pliant body and smelling the musk of her desire. He told his coachman to drive directly to his sister's home, so he would not be tempted to stray into dishonor. But he did hold her tight. He spoke clear and low into her ear. And once, he allowed himself to touch her breast by way of demonstration. He pinched her nipple and whispered of what she could do between her thighs.

And when he was nearly bursting with his own need, he opened the carriage door and stepped out while the air cooled his overheated body. He walked her to the front door, just as a gentleman ought. He handed her to his sister's butler and bowed before he withdrew.

Then he retreated to the dark interior of his carriage where the scent of her still lingered. He opened his breeches, took himself in hand, and beat out his pleasure. It wasn't enough. It wasn't close to the same, but it was all he had.

He'd never hated his title more.

CHAPTER FOURTEEN

AMBER HADN'T REALIZED it was possible to feel so many things all at once. After leaving Elliott's side, she had expected this hot, uncomfortable feeling to go away. It did not. She lay in bed in a nightrail that covered her from neck to ankle and couldn't stop thinking about what he'd said. Not just the dark whispers in the carriage about where to touch herself and how, but the rest. The admiration he had for her jewelry designs. The laughter he'd shared with her father when discussing politics. And those horrible, horrible words, "Nothing has changed for me."

Nothing? Nothing at all? Her entire life had turned on its ear. She wasn't even sleeping in the same bed, and her daydreams had deserted her. A week ago, she'd sat in the cage and dreamed of dancing with a prince. Now she had danced with...well, not the prince. The Regent was fat and married. But she'd danced with eligible bachelors who might very well offer for her hand. How could she dream about something that was actually happening? Most of her waking thoughts were occupied with the very real idea of living the rest of her life with someone who talked constantly about his horses. Or who had a mouth shaped like a frog's.

She couldn't imagine kissing most of them, let alone the things she'd already done with Elliott. How would she share a marriage bed with them? How would she share lunch with them? At least three ate like they were starving animals. They'd barely managed to fist their utensils.

And even if she could ignore all of that, who among them would allow her to still sculpt jewelry? To spend hours in the back shop carving wax?

The questions were exhausting. It was a relief to focus on Elliott's instructions as she lifted her nightrail up to her neck. She trailed her fingers slowly up her sides until she cupped her own breasts. It felt odd to do so and yet also a relief. It was nice to imagine his hands there instead of her own. She tried to mimic the way he had touched her, including the pinch to her nipple.

She felt the burst of sensation from that, but it wasn't the same. It wasn't his hands on her, and it was hard to imagine the heat of his breath and the span of his hands. Then she tried to envision any of her suitors doing the same to her. Their hands, their mouths…

That felt so wrong that she took her hands away and rolled over in bed. She wanted Elliott, and no amount of fantasy would change that. But what if she thought simply of what was here and now? Maybe her own hands could make her feel good?

She rolled over to stare grumpily at the ceiling. In truth, she didn't want it to feel as good by herself. She wanted Elliott's body on hers. She wanted what he'd said would never happen unless she became his mistress. That was not a smart choice for her, not when eligible men were interested in her. Well, not her specifically. They wanted her dowry, which put them on the same level as Lysander and Demetrius. Those were the Wolf Pack men who flirted with her while eyeing the store. If she wouldn't consider marrying them, then why was she considering the titled men who acted in the exact same manner?

Because the titled gentlemen brought something to the bargain.

They offered her a way into the *ton* and a future for her children beyond working endless nights at the Lyon's Den. Was that a bargain she should make?

The questions were crushing her again. They took away all the pleasure that she felt in touching herself. Which meant she either had to stop and go to sleep or...

Or dive into what she really wanted to fantasize. After all, she knew quite a lot about what happened between men and women from the upstairs ladies. And now, with some personal experience, her imagination had a great number of remembered details to make the experience more real. Elliott kissing her hard as she backed against the worktable. Elliott on his knees between her thighs as he pushed his fingers inside her.

He'd told her where to touch herself between her thighs. He'd told her to look for a place of extra sensation. He'd told her, and she remembered. While one hand squeezed her nipple, her other went between her thighs to mimic what Elliott had done to her. Except when that wasn't enough, she imagined his mouth there. The upstairs ladies had talked often about that. And when that wasn't enough, she thought about his manhood. She'd seen improper sketches. A great deal of improper things went through the Lyon's Den.

Her breath came short, and her back arched. It was still a pale comparison to the real man. She persevered in any event, focusing instead on the memory of his whispers next to her ear in the dark carriage. What he'd said to do. How his body had pressed so close to hers. And how she'd wanted him right then to slip his hands between her thighs and—

She quickened with a gasp. Pleasure burst through her cells, and she rocked in startled joy. But the sensations faded quickly. No man held her. No words were whispered into her ear. And though she felt a languor spread through her body, it wasn't the same.

Disappointed, she rolled onto her side and stared glumly into the darkness. Why couldn't dreams come true be exactly like the dreams?

MORNING CAME WITH a fitful sky that kept trying to rain but didn't do more than spit. She would have slept longer, but Diana woke her with a firm knock. Then, before Amber did more than crack her eyes, the woman bustled in carrying a couple more gowns that her maid had altered to fit her.

"I know it's early, but we need to capitalize on the interest created by your dowry. I've gotten us invitations to a luncheon, then a stroll around the shops, afternoon tea, followed by Hyde Park. We'll have to choose between ball invitations tonight unless you'd prefer a night at the theater."

"Why are you doing this?" If Amber had been more awake, she would have phrased the question more delicately.

Diana's eyes widened, and she set the dresses at the base of the bed. "Whatever do you mean?"

Amber sighed and sat up. "I'm very grateful, but you don't owe me anything. Your brother doesn't need me to go to any more parties." He'd probably prefer she stay completely unknown. It would be easier to make her his mistress. "You're giving up your time and your dresses, not to mention risking your reputation by sponsoring a jeweler's daughter. Why would you do that?"

Diana stared at her a long moment, then she gingerly settled down on the bed. When she spoke, it was quiet and with a great deal of candor. "I never got my own season. I'd been planning it for years, but…well, you know I married against my choice. There were a few years after the wedding to do the fashionable rounds, but Richard became sick soon after that. He was better at home this winter. Strong enough to promise me treats this Season, but he grew sick the day after we arrived."

"I am so sorry, my lady," Amber said. And she was. Diana did not have an easy life. Amber hadn't even met her husband. The man kept to his sickbed, but she had overheard enough from the staff. He was wasting away, and Diana had no choice but to wither with him.

Unless, of course, she had a girl to sponsor.

"I have accepted my life," she said as she patted Amber's hand. "But it is lovely to have a reason to go through it all with someone else."

"Isn't there a family member—" Amber began, but Diana rolled her eyes.

"Gwen would rather cut off her own legs than go dancing. And as for our other sister, Lilah, well she's a by-blow, and everyone knows it. We can't sponsor her. It just isn't done."

"Neither is sponsoring me."

Diana nodded, her expression thoughtful. "Well, no one knows about you, so there's that. Maybe I can find a way." Then she abruptly brightened. "But that's thoughts for next Season. I'm interested in this one. Are you ready to discuss the men?"

Amber frowned. "What men? Which men?"

"Well," Diana said as she waggled her eyebrows. "I've created a list." She pulled several sheets of foolscap from her pocket and set them on the coverlet between them. "I hope that wasn't presumptuous of me. This has to be overwhelming, and I thought I'd help you sort the wheat from the chaff."

Amber stared down at the list. Diana had written nearly two dozen names along with their full title and pedigree. She'd also made notes as to their per annum income and their habits, which included interest, faults, and detractors. Under one man's name, she'd written, "Laughs like a donkey."

Amber pointed to it. "Truly?"

"Oh, yes. It might not bother you, but listening to that braying night and day would put me off my food. You'll have to let me know when you meet him. He'll be at Hyde Park today and has written Elliott requesting an introduction."

So formal. So very different from what she was used to. "What does your brother think?"

"I doubt he knows. I've been corresponding with his secretary. Elliott won't get involved until it's time to negotiate the marriage settlement."

Naturally. She should have realized that, but there was so much to remember. "What do you think?"

Diana grinned. "Well, that's the question, isn't it? It depends on what you prefer."

So began a delightful hour spent in gossip. Diana had plenty of tales of who was accounted sensible, who was not, and who was overly fond of hunting or had bad breath. Some of the gentlemen on the list frequented the Lyon's Den, and several more had been the topic of conversation inside the Den. The two ladies talked with animation and much laughter, and Amber began to see the girl Diana must have been before her forced marriage to a sickly man, back when she'd been full of life. She was undoubtedly a beautiful woman when she smiled.

But then Diana gasped as she looked at the clock on the mantle. "Goodness, we must get dressed now if we're to make the luncheon. But I must send the acceptances for tonight. Will it be the theater or the ball?"

"Which one will your brother likely attend? Do we need his escort?"

"We do not, and I think he'll be at the ball. By showing up at Almack's last night, he announced that he's looking for a bride. Much easier to hunt for a woman at the balls."

Good thing that Diana had no idea how much her words cut

straight through Amber's heart. Not only was Elliott unwilling to wed her, but he was now hunting for a different girl, one with a pedigree and a family of political influence. She wondered if he had a list akin to the one Diana had made. One where the girls were ranked in order and noted with things about teeth and unappealing habits.

He probably did, and Amber would do well to remember it.

"Let's go to the theater," she said abruptly. "My feet will be aching after everything this afternoon."

Diana flashed her a sympathetic smile. "I believe that's for the best. He needs a political wife, you realize."

This was not a discussion she wished to have with Elliott's sister. "He explained it in painful detail last night."

Diana's expression took on horrified look. "He wasn't cruel, was he? You haven't developed tender feelings for him, have you?"

Tender feelings? No. More like furious, angry, lustful, achingly frustrated feelings. But she wasn't going to say that to Diana. "Let's have no more talk of your brother. He is out of my thoughts and replaced by at least a dozen other gentlemen." In the last hour, they had pared down Diana's list to fourteen possibilities, but three of special interest.

"Excellent," Diana said with a bright smile. "Now hurry and dress. We have no time at all!"

CHAPTER FIFTEEN

T HE DAY WAS exhausting. Endless rounds of polite discussion, proper posture, and veiled jabs frayed Amber's nerves. She knew that women were dangerous, spiteful creatures. The ladies' side of the Lyon's Den had taught her that. When she had helped with the dancing lessons or filled in occasionally at the women's gaming tables, she had been treated with disdain if not outright cruelty. But she had assumed that was because to them, she'd been no more than a servant.

Now she was one of them, or so they thought, and the things that they said to her were even more cruel, more hurtful, and more bizarre. They complimented her dress as a means to insult her. More than one woman praised her for being so economical as to refashion an old gown such that only the most discerning viewer could see that it wasn't new. Others told her not to worry about being so long in the tooth. Twenty-five wasn't old, but they seemed to think she was already in her dotage. And they seemed to have an obsessive interest in her freckles. She'd never really bothered with them before. Since she spent so much time indoors, she gloried in bright days when she could lift her face to the sun. Those days had marked her cheeks, apparently, and now she was given advice on how to cover them with cosmetics or bleach them right off her face.

Diana had counseled her to smile and ignore every single word, but it was hard when the petty sniping came as a constant barrage. She did her best to focus on the gentlemen in her environs. Almost all of them were on Diana's list, though some were already crossed off. Those who remained husband possibilities behaved in a perfectly acceptable manner. But she had no idea what they were like in private, because she was never, ever alone with them or anyone else.

She never thought she'd miss the quiet times in the cage where the only sound was Lina's abacas and the muted sounds of gameplay from the main floor. Right now, she longed for those very late times when all but the most dedicated gamblers had departed. The dealers worked with careful efficiency, and everyone else waited in silence for the night to end.

"Miss Gohar, may I introduce you to…"

"Let me tell you about my collection of rare Azawakhs. You'd think they were regular greyhounds, but…"

"What a sickly shade of yellow that is. You really shouldn't wear…"

On and on it went throughout the afternoon. By the time they'd finished strolling in Hyde Park, Amber's head was throbbing. She had only an hour to rest before dressing for the theater, and she planned to spend it on her bed with a wet towel over her face. No one would be allowed to say one word to her because, good Lord, how the *ton* liked to talk!

She was just starting to relax into her pillow when a soft knock sounded on her door.

Too exhausted to hide her irritation, Amber groaned by way of response. Diana didn't seem to notice, however, as she stuck her head into the bedroom.

"Bad news," she said. "Richard has taken a turn for the worse. I won't be able to go to the theater with you tonight."

Amber sat up. "Oh, dear. Is there anything I can do?"

"Not at all. Just have a good time without me."

"But I can't go without you. Let me stay here—"

Diana shook her head. "You can't. Not after rushing out so precipitously last night. People would begin to talk."

"But—"

"Trust me. You need to go, but you also need a companion."

Elliott? She couldn't even say his name out loud, but her heart was already thumping in anticipation.

"My mother has agreed to do it. She loves flirting with Lord Portham for all that's he's fat as a cow. Just make sure she lets you talk with Portham's son. He's quiet, but he's counted quite clever."

Amber nodded, her heart slowing to a depressed ka-thump. "I would be happy to stay here with you."

Diana gave her a sad smile. "Part of learning to be a society wife is learning what invitations to accept, reject, and forget. You cannot forget this one. Not even if your head is pounding, and your feet feel like they're five sizes too large."

"How do you know?"

"Because I was right beside you all day, and I feel the same way."

Actually, Amber had meant how did she know which invitations to accept, reject, or forget, but she supposed that would come with experience. "Perhaps I could read to your husband—"

"That's my duty, I'm afraid because I'm married and you've yet to cross that particular bridge. So get ready. Mother will be here early just so she can force you to change everything you're wearing, then borrow your jewelry."

Amber frowned. "I will not let her wear the lion. It's how everyone knows me. They keep talking about the lion in my hair, the roar of my beauty, the..." She waved her hands. She really didn't want to remember any of the dreadful puns she'd heard this day.

"Trust me," Diana said with a laugh. "They'll remember you

without it, but create some sort of lie about how special it is to you. Given to you by your sick but now recovered grandmama."

Oh yes. They'd been telling everyone that good news had awaited Amber after rushing home from Almack's last night. Her grandmother was on the mend, all was well, and she felt very silly for her emotional display. Most gentlemen had patted her hand and told her those excess emotions were a plague of the fairer sex, and they forgave her for being female.

Blech. She hated condescending men.

"It is special to me," Amber said softly. "It reminds me of who I am."

"You are Miss Amber Gohar, who is about to make a brilliant match. Mother may plague you tonight, but she does add extra support to your respectability. Try not to strangle her if she becomes too obnoxious."

"I'm sure she'll be fine." She wasn't at all sure, but Diana had enough to worry about. Amber didn't want to add more.

"Excellent. I'll leave you to it then. And do try to have a little fun! Life can get dreadful very fast."

There was weight to her last words, and though Diana left with a smile, there was a darkness in her that was painful to see. Amber might struggle beneath the weight of her dream come true, but Diana's life was immeasurably worse married to a sick, old man and plagued by a wastrel stepson who was larger and scarier. Amber feared for Diana, but there was nothing she could do about it now. She had to focus on getting through tonight with the dowager Lady Byrn. Especially since Diana's maid came to help her dress.

The gowns were beautiful, of course, and Amber selected a light green one so pale as to appear white. It was a measure of her mood. She felt worn down and bleached out. She almost didn't wear the lion hairpiece, but everyone was accustomed to seeing it, so she allowed the maid to put it in. She made it downstairs just after Lady Byrn arrived and found the woman interrogating Titan...er, Lucifer in the front hallway.

"I don't remember seeing you here before," the lady was saying.

The man bowed deeply before her. "I am new to the household, my lady. Here to help out for a short time."

"Well, I don't approve. You look very dangerous, and I don't like dangerous people around my daughter."

Then she ought to look into Geoffrey rather than harass the man hired to protect Diana. But Amber couldn't say that. Instead, she hurried down the stairs with a warm smile. "Lady Byrn, how beautiful you look."

The lady turned with a harrumph as she inspected Amber from head to toe. Then she shook her head. "That won't do. That won't do at all." The lady waved her hand at her in an imperious gesture. "Upstairs. I won't go to the theater with you unless you are properly attired."

Of course, she wouldn't. Hadn't Diana warned her that Lady Byrn would require her to change? She bowed her head and forced herself to say placating words. "I would welcome your advice, my lady." Then as she straightened, she caught Lucifer's surprised expression. Did he think she wouldn't give in? A day ago, she might have stood her ground. Today, she cared so little for her dress that she could wear sackcloth and barely notice.

Amber went upstairs, and after a half-hour of criticism, Lady Byrn gave in with little grace. "I see now why you picked that dress. It is the best of a bad lot, but that lion in your hair doesn't match. Though..." she said as if she had just thought of it. "It would look lovely in mine. I have always been able to wear gold to perfection."

"I did draw a few peacock designs for you." Amber opened her sketchbook to the appropriate pages. "There are quite a few possibilities there. You can choose whichever one you like. I'm sure if you dropped a word to your son, he would have it made for you as a birthday gift."

The lady's eyes brightened as she began a study of the designs, eventually picking out the most expensive. "Don't you think that one is the best?" she asked.

"You are quite right. That would suit your eyes." Then Amber gently pulled out the page and handed it over. "Just give that your son. He'll know just what to do." Then she gasped as she gestured to the clock. "Oh my! I hadn't realized I had dawdled so long. My lady, you must forgive me for making us tardy. Please, I'm ready to go now. Let us be off before Lord Portham thinks we've forgotten him." Then she managed to hurry, bully, and apologize in such rapid succession that they were in the carriage a few moments later.

If she'd been alone, Amber would have grinned. All those days helping the dancing master had taught her how to manage angry society women, and Lady Byrn was no different. However, Amber did have to listen to a lecture on how to behave at the theater. The list went from the excruciatingly obvious, all the way through to most subtle forms of observation, the most interesting of which was to watch a man's feet as he spoke. "Men lie with their mouths and hands all the time, and no one can tell," the lady said, "but if the feet twitch or are placed to run away, then they are certainly hiding something."

That was an idea worth exploring, and so she resolved to keep half an eye on gentlemen's feet tonight. It would at least alleviate some of the boredom while listening to tales of their latest hunt.

They found Lord Portham's box quickly, went through the usual introductions of the eight people already there—a mixture of eligible ladies and their chaperones—and then Amber found herself seated in the back of the box with an excellent view of Lady Byrn as she did indeed flirt outrageously with Lord Portham. Amber would have preferred a view of the stage, but perhaps no one would notice if she closed her eyes and took a nap. Her first trip to the Theatre Royal—and sitting in a box, no less—and all she could think about was her bed. How sad that this was her dream come true.

The tragedy had just started when Lord Portham's son stepped into the box. He apologized in low whispers for his delay, then sat in the only chair available, the one right next to her. This produced a number of hard glares from the eligible ladies as he, apparently, was the reason they were all here. Lady Byrn for her part, shot Amber a triumphant look before turning back to discuss a new breed of hound with Lord Portham.

Had the lady foreseen just this circumstance and maneuvered the situation to Amber's benefit? It appeared so, and her estimation of the lady increased. Meanwhile, the gentleman in question introduced himself as Mr. Christopher Jupp and settled beside her with a barely audible sigh.

"It's not a very good view, is it?" he muttered.

"No. But the chatter is so loud in here, I can barely hear the actors' voices anyway."

He shook his head. "Pity. Kean's performance is very good."

"You have seen it before?"

He grinned. "A few times in a friend's box closer to the stage."

He must have wealthy friends, indeed. They spoke quietly for a while, pausing to catch what he deemed the best parts of the play. The audience did settle in those moments when Kean appeared, but it was by no means as absorbing an event as she had thought it would be. Though to be fair, *Richard III* was not her favorite play, and Mr. Jupp was an interesting man. He was a man of books, speaking earnestly of the difference between plays and epic poetry. When she encouraged him, he was able to discuss how Shakespeare's *Hamlet* came originally from an old folktale *Hamblet,* and then he blushed and apologized for blathering on.

It was such a relief from hearing about dogs that she reassured him she was interested. It wasn't a lie. He talked about characters in such a sweeping way that she found it sparked her artist's mind. How would she sketch a sad Hamlet as opposed to a happy one? And Hamblet was a new idea entirely. She didn't create cameos, but the idea of sculpting famous characters was a fascinating thought. They discussed it quite avidly at the intermission. And though she didn't say she created jewelry, she became quite open about her sketches.

And while she and Mr. Jupp discussed the play he was penning, the other ladies scowled at her for monopolizing his time. All except Lady Byrn, who winked at her before skillfully stepping between her and the other women. That left her and Mr. Jupp not quite alone but certainly cut off the others as they continued to talk.

She liked this man. And though he wasn't Elliott, and he certainly didn't look at her in the same way, he was pleasant to talk to, his ideas inspired her, and his feet were aimed straight at her. A win in three categories, and that was more than any man had accomplished so far.

Then gentlemen began knocking at the box door. They were barely three minutes into intermission, but this was the time the *ton* visited one another. The influx of bodies was hard to manage, and Amber found herself pressed up against the front side of the box, fearing that she might topple over onto the floor below. Mr. Jupp grabbed her elbow, and she clutched his forearm. How absurd! If one went over, the other would as well.

They looked at each other then, both flinching aside as the lady nearest them gestured wildly with her fan. They recovered quickly, but the hilarity of it all had them catching each other's gazes and fighting not to laugh. That didn't work, and soon the two of them burst into giggles.

It was a sweet moment as Amber began to relax among the *ton*. It was also the moment of her undoing. One of the gentlemen whipped around, his voice loud as he called out.

"I know that laugh! It's most distinctive."

Amber's eyes widened. No one had ever said that her laugh was distinctive, but she supposed everyone made their own particular sound. That gentleman, for example, was a regular at the Lyon's Den. She knew his voice very well. He often stayed late when the Den was less crowded, and workers like her were left to chat amongst themselves. She had friends in the Den, people who made her laugh, and so he must have heard her. He absolutely did point his finger straight at her as he crowed. "It's you! Thisbe Gold! The most beautiful gel in the Lyon's Den. Whatever are you doing here?"

Amber felt her jaw drop and her breath catch. She was exposed. Worse, the declaration had come in a voice that carried throughout the box, if not the whole theater. Cold chills shivered through her body, and panic clutched at her throat. But also, a sense of inevitability sank to her belly. What had she been thinking? Dreams did not come true. Not unless they were nightmares. One where everyone stared at her in horror.

She knew she ought to say something. Deny it, if nothing else. But the shock of having her identity shouted like that left her addled. And the wash of conflicting emotions made her tongue thick and her mind lost amid the chaos of feelings.

But Lady Byrn did not have such difficulty. "Just how much have you imbibed, Mr. Walsh?" she demanded, her voice even louder than his had been. "Speaking of such a thing among polite company! It is bad enough that you choose to frequent such a disreputable location, but do not ascribe your hallucinations to anyone else." Then she strode over to Amber's side, grabbed her arm in a vise-like grip, and hauled her forward. "This is my daughter's dear friend from school, and you owe her the sincerest apology."

Mr. Walsh was not drunk, though he certainly had been drinking. He blinked as he stared at her. His mouth screwed up into a mean kind of smile. "Are you sure, my lady? As you say, I do frequent disreputable places, but I never forget a face. Certainly not one as lovely as hers."

He wouldn't have seen her face...much. That was why her father insisted she wear a scarf to cover her features. But it got hot in the summer and sometimes late at night, she would discard the covering. He could have seen her then. He certainly could have heard her laugh.

Mr. Jupp stepped forward, his tone cold. "You can't tell your own mother's face when you've been drinking, Rodney. Apologize and take yourself off until you've sobered up."

That was gallant of Mr. Jupp, and Amber flashed him a look of gratitude. And in that moment, she found her voice. "You seemed to have mistaken me for someone else, sir. In this darkened theater, I imagine I look rather common."

"No, miss, you do not," the man said. But before Lady Byrn could castigate him again, Mr. Walsh sketched a mocking bow. "But my eyes have been playing tricks upon me lately. I do apologize for my error."

"You are forgiven, sir," Amber managed.

"Provided you make pains to explain your error to others who might be equally confused," Lady Byrn said harshly.

Mr. Walsh opened his mouth to speak more, but he wasn't given the chance. Mr. Jupp released Amber's arm to manhandle Mr. Walsh out the door. Another gallant move, except that it left Amber alone while everyone in the box looked at her with open speculation. And not just them, but people in the nearest box as well. And probably from the floor below and boxes all the way around the theater. At least that's how it felt.

She tried to tell herself that it had been bound to happen. She had lived in London for most of her life. It had been foolhardy to think no one would recognize her. But those words were useless to her. She felt awkward and miserable, standing there as the center of attention. In her dreams, people had always looked at her and exclaimed over her beauty, her poise, and her laugh. Now, they were remembering her laugh, analyzing her beauty, and no doubt sneering at her lack of poise.

After a day of being subtly insulted at every turn, this was the moment that crushed her. And though Lady Byrn did her level best to distract everyone, the other ladies soon began whispering behind their fans. Amber had worked the ladies' room at the Den enough to know what they were saying. They were forever attaching her name to the place, whether it was true or not. The speculation alone would damn her in many people's eyes. That it was entirely true only made it worse.

But Lady Byrn was nothing if not a society maven. She deftly introduced a new topic of conversation, involved as many of the girls as possible with the eligible gentlemen, and did her best to distract everyone from what had just occurred.

It didn't erase what had happened, but it helped. Amber was soon brought into a discussion of the best weather for a fox hunt. Also, the best attire for a fox hunt. And of course, the best dogs for a fox hunt.

Mr. Jupp returned just before the end of the intermission. His face was flushed, and his expression serious. Amber blew out a sigh of relief and hoped to renew their discussion, but she didn't have a chance. She had monopolized him too much that evening, and the other ladies grabbed him up the moment he entered the box.

He danced attendance upon them while she was left to hear about the best food for dogs who would be used in a fox hunt. And was never more grateful than when the tragedy began again. But Mr. Fox Hunt, as she now called him, had taken Mr. Jupp's seat. She was left to listen to him prattle on about hunting while the rest of the play progressed.

It was miserable, and she counted the moments until the first play was over all the while praying that Lady Byrn had no interest in staying for the farce. Another three hours of this would break what was left of her.

Thankfully, Lady Byrn declared a headache, and Amber leaped to her feet to help the poor woman to their carriage. But in this, they were forestalled as Mr. Jupp did one last gallant thing. He asked if he might escort her around Hyde Park tomorrow afternoon.

Amber was so stunned that she couldn't even stammer out a coherent reply. He was a good man, and she had just enlisted him in duping the rest of the *ton*. It was horrible of her, and yet, what could she do? If she confessed all, she would shame Lady Byrn and her entire family.

So Amber nodded, tears swimming in her vision. Lady Byrn had no such problem, of course. She loudly exclaimed that it would be a delight for him to take her to the park. She made sure everyone there knew that Amber had claimed him for tomorrow at the Fashionable Hour. And then she whisked Amber out the door.

Done. Or nearly done as it took twenty minutes to make their way through the crowd and finally climb into the carriage. But finally, they were inside the dark and headed to Diana's home. Amber could at last close her eyes and exhale. This day's horrible round of parties and theatre was finally over. But the moment the carriage began moving, Lady Byrn snapped her fan hard on Amber's knee. When Amber jumped in surprise, the lady spoke with loud, angry words.

"Out with it."

"My lady?"

"The truth, and all of it without exception."

"But…" What should she say?

"Do you think me a fool? I know you are no dear friend of Diana's. You have somehow gotten my son, my daughter, and now me involved in your havey cavey schemes. I will know the truth of it now, or I shall stop this carriage right here, toss you into the street, and be done with you completely. Do not think I won't."

Amber believed her. Lady Byrn was livid, and Amber was out of convenient daydreams to fill in the silence.

Oh, who was she kidding? Her fictions weren't daydreams. They were lies, and she had been telling them to herself and everyone else for so very, very long. And now she was well and truly caught.

CHAPTER SIXTEEN

E LLIOTT DAMNED HIMSELF for a fool. He'd spent the day doing a
dozen important things. He'd handled a letter from his steward
regarding the management of their family estate. He'd met with
members of his political party and had drinks with members of the
opposition. Then he'd attended balls and danced with girls he might
marry, all while thinking about Amber.

No matter what he did, she was in his thoughts. The image of her,
the smell of her, and the sound of her laugh. He thought about her
words and the feel of her body pressed against his. And when he
cursed himself for thinking so carnally, his mind wandered to her
solution with Baron Easterly. He thought of her jewelry and wondered
who sported designs from her hand.

When the whispers about her identity as Thisbe Gold reached his
ears, he finally had an excuse to see her. One that had him using his
key to slip into Diana's dark house. He tiptoed upstairs and pressed his
ear to Amber's bedroom. When he heard the unmistakable sound of
tears, he knocked as quietly as could be managed, then slipped inside.

He heard her sit up with a gasp and was quick to whisper. "It's me,
Elliott. I came to see if you are all right."

He heard her blow out a relieved breath as she lit a candle. The warm glow filled the space, and he was able to see her face clearly. Her eyes were red-rimmed, and her skin was blotchy, but she held her chin high.

"What are you doing here, Elliott?"

He wanted to wrap her in his arms. He wanted to hold her as she sobbed out her troubles so that he could fix everything for her. But he was already well beyond the bounds of propriety just for sneaking into her room.

"I heard about what happened at the theater." He took a step forward and offered her his handkerchief. "What can I do?"

She took it and wiped her eyes. He used the time to sit down at the base of her bed. He would not leave her when she was this upset.

"Sometimes, a woman just needs to cry. There is nothing to fix, no one to punish, and nothing to say. Unless you mean to chastise me for being stupid."

Elliott frowned. "You are not stupid. I am hard-pressed to find a smarter woman."

"Oh, there are quite a few who are cleverer than I," she said dryly. "Your mother, for one."

A cold chill ran down his spine. "What has she done?"

Amber shrugged, and he was momentarily distracted by the shift of her breasts beneath the high-necked nightrail. "She has been clever, Elliott. She knows I am not Diana's dear friend."

"Did Diana say something?"

She shook her head. "Mr. Walsh said something, and though she covered, she was smart enough to know it was the truth."

"I will set him straight," Elliott growled. He was startled by the violence in his own voice. She was, too, because she pulled back from him with wide eyes.

"He was right," she said firmly. "I am Thisbe Gold."

"You are Amber Gohar," he said clearly. "And I will challenge anyone who says differently."

She threw up her hands. "Then you might as well draw a pistol on me because I told her the truth. I told her who I am and that you needed me for your resolution to help the veterans."

He held his breath. "Anything else?" Did she speak of how he had kissed her or that he had asked her to be his mistress? Had she told his mother of the shameful way he had treated her?

"I told her I make jewelry." Her lips curved. "I offered to make the peacock I designed for her, and she became very interested in that."

"That is no surprise," he said as the clench in his belly eased. "Be sure that she pays you a fair price. She will try to—"

"I don't need your advice on how to get paid." Her tone was tart and angry, and he flushed at her words. He was completely in the wrong here. He shouldn't have tried to make her his mistress, he shouldn't have brought her into his family to be harassed by his mother, and he definitely shouldn't be here in her bedroom. Yet, he couldn't make himself leave.

"Why were you crying?"

She leaned back against the headboard. "Have you ever had a dream come true only to find it was nothing like you expected?"

He frowned. "As a boy, I wanted to swim the channel only to discover that the water is really cold. I barely got two feet before coming back."

She smiled. "Why did you want to swim the Channel?"

He tried to remember, but it was so long ago. "I thought it would be fun to swim to France." He squeezed her ankle through the coverlet. "But I don't think that's what you meant."

"In a way, it is. I have always dreamed of dancing among the *ton*. Of being one of you, of meeting a handsome prince, and falling desperately in love."

"That's still possible, I suppose—"

"I am among you, Elliott, and it's nothing like I thought." She looked up at him, her eyes large and dark in the dim light. "It's hard."

She didn't need to explain more. He knew how difficult it was to move through the *ton*, especially as an unmarried woman. He had heard his sister Gwen complain often of petty cruelties and vicious gossip, and she had been born to her position. "I will be more public in your support. Perhaps if I take you to a ball tomorrow—"

"No," she said softly. "Your family has already given me more than I deserve. You wanted me to make a brooch. We should go tomorrow—"

"You deserve respect. You deserve to enjoy yourself without being harassed. You deserve to dance with your prince and fall desperately in love." His words were vehement. He hesitated, but somehow the question came out anyway. "And have you found someone? It isn't Mr. Walsh, is it?"

Her lips curved. "That drunkard? No. But Mr. Jupp seems nice."

He was. A sober poet of a man. Nothing objectionable, and in fact, they might have a great deal in common. Elliott hated him. It was irrational. He wanted Amber for himself, and everyone else be damned. But that wasn't what was best for her, and so he forced himself to stand up.

"I should not be in here."

"Is it always so mercenary?" she asked abruptly. "Does no one fall in love?"

"Scores fall in and out of love all the time," he said. "But none marry." Then honesty forced him to admit the truth. "There are a few love matches every Season."

"And do they stay in love? Do they live happily ever after?"

He opened his mouth to assure her that, of course, they did. It was what she wanted to hear. Instead, he sighed. "Do you want me to lie to you?"

"No."

"Many love matches fail, but there are a few that seem based on mutual respect." He swallowed as he took a step closer to her. "I am looking for that in my marriage. One where I respect her, and she me. We can work together to achieve the same goal."

"Your political career." It wasn't a question, but he answered it anyway.

"Yes."

"And did you find her tonight? Do you have a list of eligible ladies who will fit your plans?" She gestured over the writing desk. "That's Diana's list for me."

He saw that it was crumpled and tossed into a corner of the writing desk. "You don't like her suggestions?"

Amber looked up at him, and in the candlelight, her eyes seemed to glow. "It's not falling desperately in love, is it? It's not happily ever after if it's planned like a military campaign."

"So, you cry because your dreams aren't coming true the way you want them to?" He wasn't chastising her for that. He was merely trying to understand, and her nod took away his confusion.

"I am such a fool," she whispered.

"Actually," he said as he leaned against the mattress, "It makes you remarkably clearheaded to both feel the emotion and know its cause." He touched her cheek. It wasn't wet, but her skin was heated, and her eyes still swollen. "I cannot think of many men or women who understand themselves so well."

She snorted. "Then, you have remarkably stupid friends."

"On the contrary. I find you remarkably intelligent. And given that my sister Gwen is a great bluestocking, that is high praise indeed." She didn't respond to that, and in time, he said what he really wanted to say. "I want to make this better for you."

Her lips curved. "Will you fall desperately in love with me?"

His gut clenched, and his heart thudded hard in his throat. "Amber..." Her name came out in an anguished sigh. She was not a possible wife for him, and yet his blood surged at the thought.

She waved him aside. "No, no. It is a silly dream."

He pulled her face back to look at him. "It is not silly. I want you. Can you not tell?"

She frowned, and her head moved back and forth in slow denial.

He should not do this. He had already taught her too much. But he did not stop himself as he took hold of her hand and slowly, gently brought it to the heated bulge behind his falls. The press of her hand was electric as sensation burst through his body. He steeled his spine so as not to thrust forward at her touch. And when he spoke, his voice was rough with need.

"Do you know what that is?"

"I... Yes." She wet her lips, and he could not stop looking at the glisten of moisture on her mouth.

He forced himself to release her hand and was grateful when she did not pull away. She used her fingers to measure the length of him. It was curiosity, he knew, but it felt like the touch of a talented courtesan. She inflamed him. And while he controlled his breath, his hips surged forward into her hand.

"Is this all right?" she asked as she pressed back, adding resistance to his thrust.

The candlelight showed him the flash of desire in her eyes. "Minx," he said as he teased her back. "You know I want it. I have told you so."

"I have heard about it," she said absently, her gaze focused on what she did as she outlined the tip of his cock. "The upstairs ladies talk a great deal about it."

"I shudder to imagine."

"Is yours considered large?"

Such a question! "Above average, I should think."

She grinned at him. "Isn't that what all men say?"

"Yes, I suppose so." The sight of her grin made his heart light. Indeed, everything about her made him happier, though it made no sense whatsoever. He might have thought about it more deeply. He was a man who considered such things. But he had no more thoughts as she deftly unbuttoned his clothing and began to peel the fabric away.

"Amber." He groaned. "This is not proper."

"Neither am I," she said bluntly. "And if you don't mind, I should like to see it for myself."

He didn't mind. He wanted it desperately, and she knew it. He didn't help her free him from his clothing. Instead, he touched her cheeks, her hair, and the sweep of her ear.

"You don't need to do it. This is not why I came here."

"But I want to." She abruptly changed her position on the bed, coming forward to sit on her knees. He stood with his knees pressed against the mattress. She inspected his cock from all angles, then she looked up at him. "I would like to experience a little." She touched him with tentative fingers and curiosity. But while the blood roared in his ears, she began to grip him more firmly and squeeze the head.

His hand wove into her hair, and his other gripped the bedpost. His buttocks tightened, but he didn't thrust. He didn't want to frighten her.

"Amber," he groaned. "You don't know what this does to a man." He was holding onto control by the barest thread.

"Does it make him fall in love?"

He swallowed, and his heart squeezed in his chest. "You know it doesn't. It makes him hunger. It makes me want you such that I cannot think of anything else."

"That's not love." She spoke as if she already knew the truth but needed to keep repeating it to herself. It was a way to remind herself that this wasn't what she wanted. And yet, she kept touching him. And when her head bowed, and she took a tentative lick across his head, he lost all rational thought.

He groaned and swayed toward her. She held him firm, and he thrust through her hand and into her mouth. And while he was stifling his moan, she swirled her tongue around him. Such a glorious feeling, and then she made it better. She sucked him. A quick pull, but he went with the motion, thrusting inside her mouth until she completely engulfed him.

His blood roared. Heat and wet pleasure. All wound together while her hand fluttered across his thighs and between his legs to touch his balls.

He gasped beneath a tidal wave of desire. He pulled back, unwilling to abuse her even more, though she fought him with a suction that tore at his sanity. He escaped her hold and fumbled for the handkerchief. But he was too slow, and she had him completely unraveled.

He erupted like a boy with his first woman. He caught most of it, saving her from embarrassment. Or perhaps he was saving himself, because she watched with rapt interest.

He released into his own hand. His breath came in raw gasps as he leaned hard on the bedpost. She helped steady him with hands braced at the top of his thighs. He was shuddering against her, and the smell of her excitement mingled with his own.

He stood there, letting the last of the release roll through his body. He saw her growing curiosity as she watched him. Her nipples were pebbled beneath her nightrail, and her hair fell about her shoulders in glorious temptation.

Such a contradiction. She was innocent in practice and yet knowledgeable. She spoke boldly of what she wanted and yet dreamed of love like a schoolgirl. She knew that a man's lust wasn't love, and yet, when she looked at him, it was as if stars filled her eyes.

"I would like to sculpt that," she whispered as she looked up at him.

"What?"

"You. Your chest heaving, your hips moving. Did you know, your neck tightens with every pulse? It is like you strain against a great weight, but there is bliss in your eyes."

He stared at her. "So poetic," he murmured, and suddenly he wanted to see what she saw in him. Why had she picked him for her adoration? For her explorations? He wanted to see her sculpture and yet she could not do such a thing. "Swear to me you will not even sketch it. Nothing, Amber. Not even in your most private moments."

She blew out a breath. "No one would see it but me." Then she looked up. "I have sketched from statues before, but nothing compares to you. Alive. So strong. So…" She pressed her palm to his belly. "It was beautiful."

He shook his head, still dazed. "No one has ever called me beautiful." Then he touched her face. "You take my breath away."

He kissed her then. How could he not? She had brought him not only bliss but also poetry. She made him think about love when he had dismissed the thought years ago as childish. And she made him want to give her everything, his wealth, his protection, and yes, even his love. But that wasn't possible for a man with a title. So, he gave her what he could.

He gave her pleasure.

He kissed her until she was breathless. And he pinched her nipples through her nightrail and swept the gown up past her hips. He stroked her legs, and he pressed his mouth to her belly. And when he thought of licking between her thighs, his mouth watered with need.

But she was already whimpering with every breath. Her body was alive and not under her control. He would not risk her making noise. Not for his own sake. He deserved to be beaten to a bloody pulp for what he was doing with her. But he would not have her shamed.

He slipped his hand between her thighs as he captured her mouth with his. He caught her cries as he thrust his fingers inside her. And when he stroked her nub, her legs spread wider. How he wanted to seat himself there now. He wanted to plow into her and plant his seed. Their children would have artist's hands and her frank wonder as they looked at the world.

He thought of that as he pumped his fingers into her. And he thought of her belly swelling as he thrust against her nub. And when she cried into his mouth, he caught her sounds and memorized the feel of her coming apart beneath him. And suddenly, he daydreamed about love and happily ever after. How wonderful would it be to do this with her every night? To wake with her in the morning as she nuzzled against him in her sleep?

He would learn to see what she did when she drew flowers or lions. And together, they could talk of things that had never entered his adult thoughts. Poetry. Beauty. Love.

She settled beneath him. He eased her nightrail down and covered her once again. He smelled her musk and memorized that, too, especially as she looked at him with dazed, happy eyes. Then she opened her mouth to say something. He couldn't let that happen. Not if her words were the ones simmering in his mind. Words that would burn them both, because they couldn't be taken back.

So, he kissed her hard and fast rather than hear them. And he kept kissing her until she lost whatever it was she might have said. And when he finally eased back, he dropped his forehead to hers.

"Don't speak," he said. "I have to leave now, and it's best if we're both quiet."

She stilled, frozen for a breath, maybe two. Then she nodded. He could feel her retreat into herself as her hands slipped away.

"I have tasks tomorrow," he said. "But the morning after, I will come early for you. We will go to Lord Morthan's estate so you can see the jewelry and figure out the brooch's design."

She nodded, and he wondered if her expression was sad. He certainly felt heaviness as he returned their relationship to a business footing. He needed her to make the brooch and nothing else. He needed the jewelry that would buy him the vote he required. Then she would return to her life and he to his. Ended, except for the memories.

"I cannot marry you," he said softly, and the words broke his heart.

"I know," she said.

He straightened and cleaned up. His cock was heavy, and lust burned in him still. But he set himself and everything else in her chamber back to rights. He even blew out the candle before easing open her bedroom door and slipping out into the hallway. A few moments later, he was outside and walking briskly through the dark back to his home.

He couldn't marry her, he told himself as his steps took him steadily away from her. But he could love her. And that was the saddest daydream of all.

CHAPTER SEVENTEEN

AMBER WOKE WITH such happiness that she knew she'd been dreaming. Well, not exactly dreaming since last night had been one of her secret dreams come true. A man had crept into her bedroom and touched her intimately. He had given her such pleasure, and she had been able to explore him in a way she'd only imagined before.

The memories had her flushing and smiling into her pillow. But even as she hugged the sheets tight to her sensitive breasts, she remembered who had been the man of her dreams. Elliott had swept into her life and pulled her from her gray cage into a world of color. Elliott, who wore black and made her feel not only wanted but also understood.

Elliott would never marry her.

Her giddy happiness drained away. Last night had been another dream come true, but today was for serious thoughts. No more fantasies, only reality. Elliott had said that he would take her to Lord Morthan's country estate tomorrow morning. After that, she would make the brooch, and they would separate. He would have no more need to sponsor her, and she would have no chance to find a respectable husband.

If she meant to secure a future for herself outside of the Lyon's Den, then she needed to do it today. *Today.*

She picked up Diana's crumpled list of men and smoothed it out. She already knew her pick, but went through the list dispassionately anyway. One by one, she reviewed Diana's notes and her memories. By the time the maid brought her a cup of morning chocolate, Amber had decided on her future.

Mr. Christopher Jupp would do well enough. He was kind and poetic, which matched her own artistic needs. If she could bring him up to scratch, then they would have an acceptable life together. So resolved, she planned her campaign.

Mr. Jupp showed up late for their ride in Hyde Park. He was full of apologies even as he began to talk about the poem he had begun that afternoon. It caused him to lose track of the time and was likely the reason he sported ink stains on his shirtsleeves, but he was also in good cheer. She realized as they walked to his carriage that this would likely be how he appeared throughout their life together. Tardy and with ink stains, but still sporting a smile. She could live with that, especially since she often lost track of time while working.

The carriage was his father's and smelled of cigars, so when they disembarked at Hyde Park, she lifted her face to the sun and breathed deeply. Unfortunately, the sun was hidden behind clouds. Mr. Jupp was still talking about his poem—this time about his choices in rhyme and meter—and she listened with half an ear as she smiled at several others out for a stroll.

"I'm blathering on again," he said with an embarrassed cough. "I do apologize."

"I like the sound of your voice," she said simply, though it wasn't quite as deep or resonant as Elliott's. In fact, his voice wouldn't wrap around her in the darkness the way Elliott's could, but that brought her back to her nighttime fantasy and not to the daytime mission.

She shut her mind to daydreams and focused on the here and now. They greeted several people of the *ton* all decked out in colors bright enough to please Amber. The words they shared were unimportant because half were trite and the other half, spiteful. Best to smile prettily and look at the birds. Or mentally criticize the jewelry. That was always fun.

They'd been in the park for twenty minutes when Mr. Jupp leaned down and spoke low into her ear. "I am so sorry for how they are all staring at you. I cannot imagine what Rodney was thinking, mistaking you for that Thisbe girl. He's generally a good fellow, you know, or at least he was in school. But he's soured lately, and I am sorry he was such an idiot last night."

Amber didn't plan her next words, but once spoken, she didn't regret them. "He might be an idiot, Mr. Jupp, but he wasn't wrong."

He didn't react at first. He was too busy smiling at a passing couple. But eventually, his step hitched, and he stared down at her. "What did you say?"

She smiled at a group of five who were taking a nearby path, then spoke in a low voice. "Perhaps we could return to the carriage. I would like to show you something."

He stared at her for a moment longer and then nodded. It took another fifteen minutes to saunter back to the edge of the park, but the carriage was nowhere in sight. Just as well. She steered them past the fashionable lanes and hailed a hackney. He went along without complaint or question, and she wondered if that was also a clue as to her future. Would he always be this docile? There were advantages to an easy-going husband, but it might be exhausting being the one in sole charge of their affairs.

He finally spoke when they were in the dark carriage. His voice was low and angry. "You are Thisbe from the Lyon's Den?"

"Yes." She would not begin a marriage with a lie, though she was very aware that this could be the end of her marriage hopes.

"What do you do there?" His voice was harsh. "And how did you get into society?" The second question sounded more like curiosity than anger. She knew the first question was his real focus.

"I am not one of the upstairs ladies like you imagine. Indeed, I am not employed by the Lyon's Den at all. I work with my father, Mr. Gold."

"And what do you do for him?"

Now came the harder part, though she wasn't sure why. Perhaps because it was easy to give the name of the Lyon's Den and be rejected. It was harder to confess she crafted jewelry and have him despise it.

"My art is not one of sketching, Mr. Jupp. I make jewelry. I learned it at my grandfather's knee when his hands began to shake. And then I surpassed him in skill."

His brows rose. "Really? That is quite a claim from a woman."

"Nevertheless, it is true." She hated that most people did not think women could do much more than cook and sew. Shoes and jewelry were made by men. Bookkeeping and the management of businesses were done by men. And, of course, medicine and the running of the country, all handled by men. Unless it wasn't. Elizabeth I ruled England for seventy years. Amber loved thinking of that great woman.

Meanwhile, Mr. Jupp was not convinced. "I know nothing of jewelry making, but I would assume it's a taxing craft. The shaping of metal would require strength."

"My father handles most of the metalwork. I design the pieces and sculpt the wax." She pulled out the lion hairpiece and handed it to him. "I made that. And I have made many more besides."

He gave the piece a cursory inspection. He was not a man who noticed jewelry, and so, he had no understanding of the excellence he held. She didn't explain. He wouldn't understand the finer points of the task. She sat in silence while he turned the lion over and over in his hand. When they arrived at the Lyon's Den, she took him to the door of her father's shop and showed him inside.

Her father looked up with shock but quickly recovered. "Fine lady, good sir, how may I help—"

"This is Mr. Christopher Jupp, Papa," she interrupted. "If he asks you for my hand in marriage, I should like you to accept."

Both men stared at her. Neither had expected her to be so blunt. But after only a few days of living in society, she was tired of verbal games. She wanted the truth spoken clearly for all to understand. At least among the three of them.

Her father recovered first. He straightened, put on a broad smile, and began speaking to Mr. Jupp as he would any customer. Except, this time, he was selling his daughter.

Amber listened for a few minutes but couldn't stand it for long. Blocking out her father's pitch, she shrugged off her wrap and went into the back workroom. There, she began to sculpt another firebird.

And she purposely lost herself in the work.

She came back to the present hours later when the firebird was complete. This one was a bracelet with flames to wrap around a lady's wrist and wings that swept up her forearm. It was very good, but not great, and she prepared to destroy it as she did all her firebirds.

"Don't," her father said as he caught her hand. "Let me make this one as a wedding gift to you."

It took her a moment to separate from her art to his words. But when she did, her eyes widened in shock. "A wedding gift? He will propose?"

Her father beamed at her. "He has asked permission to pay his addresses to you, and we discussed a wedding in a month's time."

"A month!" *So soon?*

"It will be a quiet one in the country. Your grandpapa and I will be able to come, but no one else. Your association with us will have to be kept a secret."

"I do not want to keep you a secret!" she snapped. It was a hot statement, but inside, she knew the wisdom of it. Mr. Jupp was not so high up in society that he could marry a tradeswoman without damage. And she would not marry him if her children would be shunned by his family and friends. That would defeat the purpose of marrying into a title.

"It is for the best," her father said. "And he saw the wisdom in allowing you to sculpt for us." Her father grinned. "I believe he was surprised by our prices."

Amber sighed. "You exaggerated them."

"No, I did not." He came forward and wrapped her in his arms while pride rang in his words. "My daughter will be a fine lady. My grandson will have a title."

His grandson would become a baron one day, and that was something they could both celebrate. The child would have land and status. He would never have to run from his homeland like a beggar or a thief. This was her father's dream come true, if not exactly hers, and she should be thrilled.

Instead, she pressed a kiss to her father's cheek and headed to the door. She needed to get back to Diana's home before... She frowned. What were the plans for tonight? It didn't matter. There would be more from now on. If she married Mr. Jupp, she would attend balls, the theater, and even musical evenings for the rest of her life.

And even better, Mr. Jupp wore colors. She would never have to look at unrelieved black again except on the priest in church. Odd how the thought made her more depressed than when she'd been locked in the cage upstairs with no end in sight.

CHAPTER EIGHTEEN

UNLIKE MR. JUPP, Elliott arrived on time. He began by sending a note, asking her to be ready by noon for a drive to visit her distant relation in Cambridge. It was a lie, obviously, but it was a good enough excuse. She was ready when he arrived, but her ill-temper made her shrewish.

"Can't you ever wear anything but black?" she snapped by way of greeting.

He paused in the middle of his bow, then looked up with understandable surprise. "I beg your pardon?"

She flushed hot, then shook her head. "No, my lord, I beg your pardon. That was inexcusably rude of me. Your attire is perfectly acceptable, and I am horribly out of sorts."

He frowned as he stepped further into the parlor. "Should we delay? If you are unwell—"

"No! Please, let us get this visit over. I am simply anxious about seeing my cousin again after so much time. What will she think of me now?"

He was understandably confused by her statement though his words came out with sincerity.

"She will think you are an accomplished woman of grace and beauty." He flashed a quick smile. "And she will wonder what you are doing with someone of so little style." He gestured to his boring attire.

"You are too kind," she said, and the words burned in her throat. He was kind and generous. If it weren't for him, she wouldn't have danced at balls, gone to the theater, or met her future husband, Mr. Jupp. And she was being a shrew. "Please forgive me," she said miserably.

He took her hand and pressed a slow kiss to it. And when he raised his gaze, she saw deep regret. "I am entirely at fault. In everything, Miss Gohar."

She missed hearing her name on his lips. She wanted him to call her Amber as he had the other night. She wanted so many things. But this was life, not fantasy, and so she smiled and gestured out to the overcast day.

"We should leave soon before it rains."

"Yes," he murmured as he looked outside. "I had wanted to leave earlier, but I thought you might need more rest. I know your penchant for dancing until the very last note."

She and Diana had gone to another ball last night. And how ridiculous that she barely remembered it. A week ago, a *ton* party was a dream come true. Now she shrugged and recalled that though she'd danced the night through, she'd spent most of her time watching for Lord Byrn. "I didn't see you there," she said.

"I had other matters to attend to. I was securing the last votes for my resolution. A few gentlemen were wavering, so I had to press them to remain faithful."

"And were you successful?"

He nodded. "After today, I will bring it to a vote as soon as possible, and it should pass."

"I'm so glad." And she was. It meant a great deal to him, and she was pleased to be able to help. "I suppose we should get started then," she said.

He nodded and extended his hand. Together they stepped to his closed carriage. They were barely two feet out of the door when Diana's housekeeper came rushing out of the servant's entrance. She had her hat and cloak on as she hurriedly curtseyed to them both. Amber stared at the woman in surprise, but Elliott was all smiles.

"Thank you for joining us, Mrs. Hopkins. I am sure you are very busy today, and it is kind of you to spare some time."

"Oh, my lord," the lady answered, "I am happy to get a day away no matter the reason." She was bursting with smiles as she curtsied again. She was distracted for a moment when a kitchen maid rushed forward to ask her something. That gave Amber time to turn to Elliott in confusion.

Elliott must have read the question on her face, for he spoke in low tones. "It is not proper for me to escort you anywhere without a chaperone, much less outside of the city. Diana suggested Mrs. Hopkins needed a day off her feet."

"But…" How did she ask such a question? "My reputation is…" *Unimportant? Already in tatters?*

"You are a lady, Miss Gohar. And any man who treats you as something less is a cad." She could tell by his expression that he included himself in that category. He had not bothered with a chaperone that first night home from the ball. And certainly, no gentleman would slip into her bedroom at night. What they had done was decidedly improper, and yet now he was apologizing and acting as if she were a lady born.

"You never cared for propriety before," she whispered. It wasn't an accusation, merely a statement of fact.

"I did care," he said as he escorted her to the carriage. "But I found ways to hide my reprehensible behavior." He looked her in the eyes, his expression unwavering in its apology. "I was wrong, Miss Gohar. Exceedingly so."

He regretted what they had done together. That was her only interpretation. And how like a man to take his delight at night and then apologize in the morning. She didn't regret it. Indeed, she found herself revisiting the memories often. The way he touched her, the passion in his kiss, and how she'd felt when he'd stroked between her thighs. That pleasure had been beyond anything she'd ever experienced before, but even better was the tenderness in his eyes, the way he worshiped her with his lips, and the gentleness in his arms when he held her after. It never lasted long enough, but there had been long minutes when she'd stayed in his arms and felt such happiness.

Fortunately, she was not required to respond as he was handing her into the carriage. She settled beside Mrs. Hopkins and he across from them both. He was very gallant as he set rugs over their legs, and then signaled the coachman that they were ready to embark.

The horses started, and they began their journey. They were still in London when he looked at the housekeeper. "I hope I can count on your discretion, Mrs. Hopkins. I have news for Miss Gohar, but it is not to be bandied about."

"Of course, my lord," she answered. "You can't be a housekeeper for long if you don't know how to mind your tongue."

He smiled and nodded, then he looked to Amber. "I received a missive from Mr. Christopher Jupp this morning. He wishes to discuss your marriage contract. I have set the appointment for tomorrow. I believe he will then speak to you that evening. That is…" He cleared his throat. "Is this to your liking?"

Now it all made sense. Now that she was to marry Mr. Jupp, she was to be a proper woman. That involved chaperones and apologies. "It is everything that I ever wanted," she said, her voice cracking with the strain.

It was everything. And yet, her heart broke with the words. She knew now that there would never be another kiss from Elliott, another improper touch, or even a longing look. It was over because she was to marry a future baron.

Beside her, Mrs. Hopkins cheered in delight. She gave Amber her heartfelt best wishes and then she began sharing everything she'd ever heard about Mr. Jupp and his family. All of it was complimentary, and it continued for a good hour. And once she was finished with that, she began to give advice on the wedding breakfast. What to serve, how not to overwhelm the bride on the most exciting day of her life, and all sorts of other very practical, very useful suggestions. Amber listened closely and asked appropriate questions. There was a great deal to learn about being a proper woman. Things about running a household that had never entered her thoughts before. But if she were to become a baroness, then she would need to know these things. And Mrs. Hopkins was a font of information.

So she listened, learned, and tried not to let her head swim with details. And all the while, she pushed away any thought of the man sitting across from her. She would think only of Mr. Christopher Jupp and how to be a good wife to him.

They arrived at Lord Morthan's country estate to the patter of rain. Mrs. Hopkins went directly downstairs to visit with the house-keeper. Lord Byrn handed a missive to the butler, and they were immediately escorted to the library and left alone. Apparently, Lord Morthan had directed his staff to give them the privacy they required to accomplish the task.

Lord Byrn then went to open a safe hidden beneath the library floorboards. With careful hands, he brought out a tiara and bracelet to match the one that Amber's father had melted down so long ago. And then Elliott brought out a sketching book and pencils, plus wax and her carving knives. He opened a pouch and poured out the stones that would have to fit in the finished piece.

"I visited your father this morning," he said. "He gave me these for your use today."

She nodded, feeling dazed. She knew for sure that her father hadn't been the one to think ahead. That had been Lord Byrn, arranging everything.

"Thank you," she murmured.

"You are doing this for me, so it was incumbent upon me to make sure you have everything you need to accomplish the task." He looked down at the things set carefully on the library desk. "Did I forget anything?"

"This is everything." She swallowed. "Did you discuss Mr. Jupp's missive with Papa as well?"

Elliott nodded. "Yes, of course. He was very excited. He also told me how you brought Mr. Jupp there yesterday and told him your true identity." His voice lowered. "That was a risky gambit."

She lifted her chin. "I will not marry a man based on a lie."

He nodded. "I am not criticizing. Indeed, I am most impressed."

"That I am honest?" Her tone was stiff and angry.

He sighed. "You are determined to quarrel with me today. Very well, yes, I was surprised you would reveal yourself. Surely you have felt some of the backlash from Mr. Walsh's drunken statement. To tell Mr. Jupp the truth was very risky, but it seems to have paid off. According to your father, he means to let you keep sculpting in secret." He lowered his voice. "It is a heavy burden to lay on a man to hide his wife's true identity, but I believe he will honor it."

That was a lot spilling from a man who had barely spoken two words throughout the carriage ride. True, she and Mrs. Hopkins had given him few openings, but her mood was so foul that she would indeed damn him for that as well.

"You have arranged everything," she said quietly. "My tools and my marriage to a worthy man."

"Isn't that what you want?" he asked. Was there hesitation in his voice? Hope perhaps that she wanted something else?

She couldn't tell, and it didn't matter anyway. "No, Lord Byrn, this is perfect. As I said before, it is everything I have ever dreamed of."

"Including falling desperately in love?"

He would throw that back at her. He would press her into confessing that that piece was missing. She didn't love Mr. Jupp. No, the man she loved stood in front of her casually arranging matters such that she married someone else.

"Yes," she said. "I am desperately in love." With Elliott. And that truth nearly broke her right there.

She might have confessed all, but she wasn't given the time. Elliott gave her a stiff smile and then gestured to the table. "I shall leave you to it," he said. "I will be in the front parlor. Lord Morthan has some fine brandy."

She blinked in surprise. "You are leaving me alone here?"

"Your father said you never like being disturbed when you work."

That was true. But now that he was leaving, she found that she enjoyed his presence even when in such a horrible mood. She would have liked having him read nearby. She would have enjoyed smelling his scent and listening to his breath even as she grew absorbed in her work.

But that was illogical, and she didn't blame him for wanting to quit her company. So she nodded and sat down to work. He bowed and showed himself out.

And three hours later, the rain came.

CHAPTER NINETEEN

I F THE APOCALYPSE began with heavy rains, then surely this was the end of days. Elliott stared out the window of the parlor and wondered at God's cruelty. Bad enough that he had to help negotiate Amber's marriage settlement with that wholesome prick, Christopher Jupp; now he had to spend more hours in her company without touching her. Without thinking of how he longed to please her. Without slipping into the library just to watch her create something marvelous out of wax.

She was destined for someone else, and no gentleman should touch another man's wife.

If he were alone, he would drive the carriage himself despite the rain. He wanted to be back in London, where there were plenty of distractions from the delectable Amber. But he could not force his coachman to return in this weather and certainly not Mrs. Hopkins with her aching knees and feet. In truth, he did not like the idea of Amber out in this weather, either, so he stood in the parlor and glared at the rain.

There was nothing to do but think of her. And drink. He had already had too much of his host's fine brandy. Any more would have him disreputably drunk, and that would certainly have him giving in to impulses he had just this morning sworn to never indulge. Ever.

He set aside the bottle and tried to read, but his mind was on her. Supper was served, and he and Amber sat together for the meal. Her expression held despair. His was no different. She had finished the wax mold and declared it acceptable. He promised they would return to London—with her reputation intact—as soon as the rain stopped in the morning.

And he prayed it would stop because the sight of her so sad cut at him.

He tried to ask why. She was to be a future baroness. Christopher was everything she ever wanted. She'd even said she was desperately in love with him. So why did she look like she wanted to drown herself in the nearest river? But when he asked, she merely shrugged.

"I am not fond of rain."

"No one likes this kind of weather," he returned. Not when the world seemed to be an endless curtain of wet.

She merely looked at him and nodded. There was no fire in her to challenge him. No flash of humor. He had three sisters and a mother. He knew that sometimes women got into moods, and there was nothing a man could do but stay out of their way. But he didn't want to stay out of Amber's way. He wanted to hold her and tease her until he coaxed a smile from her lips. Or she told him what was wrong.

But that wasn't his place. That was Christopher's place, and he damned himself for ever stepping into the Lyon's Den where he'd met her and began this crazy situation.

"I think I shall retire early," she said. "It's too dark to work, and there's no sense in burning the candles when I am overtired anyway."

He didn't want her to go to bed. He wanted her to stay with him. It made no sense, but his world was not right when she was so unhappy.

"Good idea," he forced himself to say. "I will, likewise, retire early."

And so, the meal was quickly finished, and they both retreated upstairs to the chambers that had been prepared for them. He purposely did not bring up the brandy decanter. If he did, nothing would stop him from steadily consuming until he was completely insensate. Instead, he continued what he'd been doing downstairs. He stood at the window and stared into the darkness while his thoughts turned over and over on one topic.

Amber.

He remembered every moment they had been together. It surprised him that he dwelled as much on her laughter or the animated way she argued with him as he did the moments when he had slipped between her thighs. Somehow, she brought him out of himself. When she was happy, his heart was lighter. He looked about the world in a warmer way. And though he still focused on politics, he also noticed the sunlight on her cheeks, the curl of her hair that escaped her chignon, and the birds that she loved to look at. And when she was out of sorts, she pulled his attention out of his own misery and into hers. His burdens were nothing compared to her hurts, and that, too, was good for him. He spent too much time in his own head. It was good for him to think of someone else, to measure the world through someone else's eyes, and to be in a place that wasn't choked with men's cigars or women's perfumes. Those were the places of society, and he was sick of it.

Amber wore no perfume, and since escaping the Lyon's Den, she did not carry the acrid smell of cigars. She was clean and a true artist who created beauty out of wax and metal. And she was so vibrant in his mind, especially when he compared her to the bland girls his mother had forced on him. None of them was as intriguing as Amber.

But he would not disgrace her. He would not slip into her bedroom and attempt a seduction. She was not for him. And that made him hate everything and everyone. He didn't sleep. He didn't drink.

He just stared and grew more depressed with every tick of the clock.

"Elliott?"

At first, he thought he'd imagined the soft word. He'd been remembering how she whispered his name in the throes of passion. Surely that breathy whisper was from his own mind. But then it came again.

"Elliott?"

He spun around. She stood just inside his closed doorway. She wore a nightrail she'd borrowed from the housekeeper. Her honey-colored hair was loose about her shoulders, and her eyes looked so wide, they seemed to encompass her whole face.

"Amber? Is something wrong?" He took a step forward, but then stopped himself. She was temptation itself, but he was trying to be a moral man. He would not give in though every cell in his body pushed him to touch her, taste her, take her.

"I have come to a decision," she said, her voice surprisingly strong.

What decision did she have left? Her marriage was secure, her father was in full support, and she would become a baroness. There was no decision to be made.

"Would you like to know what it is?"

"Of course," he responded. It's what a gentleman said when a lady posed such a question.

She took a careful step into the room, then lifted her chin and looked him in the eyes. Such a bold stance. He was so busy admiring her strength that he nearly didn't hear the words.

"I have decided to be your mistress."

His body strained forward, but he would not be ruled by lust. He could not have heard her correctly.

"I'm so sorry, Amber. There was thunder over your words. Could you repeat that?"

There had been no thunder except the pounding of his heart, and her smile told him she knew he lied. Nevertheless, she didn't tease him about it. She simply took another step forward.

"I have decided I want to be your mistress," she said. "Assuming you will have me."

Have her? He couldn't stop visualizing all the ways he wanted to have her. But he forced his head to turn in a jerky denial. "You're going to get married. You said you loved him."

"I said I had fallen in love. I have. With you."

His breath caught. She did not know what she was suggesting. "I cannot give you marriage like he can. You won't be a baroness. Your children—"

"There will be no children," she said firmly. "I will not bear one out of wedlock."

Sound decision. But it wasn't relevant. "You are to marry Christopher."

She shook her head. "I know many women trapped in terrible marriages. They are treated as slaves, are routinely beaten and worse."

"Christopher would not do that to you."

"Maybe not, but if I am to have a transaction in my future, then I shall make the best bargain I can."

He nodded, seeing her logic even though most of his blood was far away from his brain. "He is the best bargain. He's the heir to a baronetcy."

"And I would be his wife who takes care of his household and raises his children. I would be paid nothing, have no control of my own money, and would have to sneak out in secret to carve jewelry that would put money in his pocket."

He couldn't argue that. "It is a respectable life."

She nodded. "Yes, it would be. But I find the transaction with you much more appealing. You would pay your mistress, yes? In baubles and a residence. That is the usual arrangement."

He swallowed. No gently reared woman should know this, but he found that he liked the way her mind worked. He liked that she knew the reality of what she said she wanted.

"Will you?" she pressed.

"Yes," he rasped. He would. Maybe not for any mistress, but for her, definitely.

"I would have control over my money. And if you displeased me, if you grew tired of me—"

"Never." The word was out before he even realized he'd spoken.

"But if the situation turned difficult between us, I would not be trapped. I could take my money and pay for my own lodging. And I would keep the money I make from my jewelry and not share it with you. It would be my income to do with as I see fit."

He shook his head. "You would not be respectable, Amber. You would be called a courtesan."

"What do I care what other people say of me? So long as I can make jewelry, and they buy it?"

He didn't have the ability to argue logic. Not with her standing in a nightrail so close. He could have it off and her on the bed within a trice. Still, he strove to keep her at bey for his own sanity. He feared that if he once broke his moral stance, he would not set her free for any reason. "Christopher will let you make jewelry."

She snorted. "I want no man in control of my work. I will make what I choose, and no husband will stop me."

"Certainly, no smart husband."

She shrugged. "I cannot guarantee the wisdom of any man, and so I will remain independent."

"And be a mistress?" He tried to put dismissal in his voice. He tried to tell her that she was making the wrong choice. She had a chance at a respectable life and children. But his words came out with hope rather than censure. "You would be my mistress."

"Yes."

He swallowed. "Because I will pay you?"

"Because I love you. The rest is simple practicality."

She loved him. She had said the words before, but he needed to hear it over and over again. She loved him. Not his title, not his respectability, not even his money. She loved *him*.

"But you deserve more," he whispered. He should not let her make this choice, but his cock was already throbbing with desire. His hands were fisted at his sides for fear they would grab her. And his mind was filled with the things he could teach her, and the ways they could pleasure each other. "You have a future with Christopher. With me, you have—"

"Independence. Choice." She took a last step forward. "And I can be with the man I love."

She kept saying that word, and his chest squeezed tight every time. He never expected love in his life. Responsibility, duty, and honorable service to his country. These were the things he'd been raised to embody. And all those potential brides that his mother had pushed into his path had been told the same thing. They would do their duties, fulfill their responsibilities, and support their country through service to their husbands. Not one would speak of love. That was the language of silly girls too young to know better.

Except Amber boldly stated she loved him. And for that, he had only one response.

"Why?"

"What?"

"Why do you love me? I have done nothing but treat you abominably."

She set her palm flat on his shirt. His cravat, coat, and waistcoat were already discarded, so there was little between her hand and his flesh but a thin layer of linen. He held still so she wouldn't leave him.

"You see me," she said. "You respect my art and my choices."

"But this is the wrong choice," he said, his voice raspy as he forced the words out. "You deserve marriage."

"I deserve to choose what I want." She lifted her face to his. "I choose you."

He wanted to deny it. He wanted to be unselfish and return her to the future that all women were supposed to want. He wanted her to have respect, children, and joy in her future. But he could not deny himself. Not when she offered herself with clear-headed determination, with logic, and desire in her eyes. And a scent that went straight to his head.

How could he deny her? He was certainly too weak to deny himself, though he tried one last time.

"What would your father say?"

She flinched at that, then shook her head. "I am five and twenty. It is time I made decisions for myself. He is not the one who will live my life. I am. And so, I have decided on you." And with that, she stretched up on her toes and pressed her lips to his.

Whatever restraint he had, broke at the first touch of her mouth on his. He had been dreaming of her lips not five minutes before, and now she was here, like a miracle come to life. She was in his arms, opening her body to his exploration, opening her heart to his desires, and opening her life for his use.

He didn't deserve it, but he could not give back the miracle. He was not strong enough for that.

He swept her into his arms and carried her to his bed. He set her down like the precious gift she was. And when she tried to bring him down with her, he held back. He touched the curve of her cheek and her brown curls. He let his gaze rove over her body, shrouded in that horrible nightrail. And he tightened his hand into the sheet beside her hip.

"Be sure, Amber. Because once I have you, I will not give you up."

She nodded. "I am sure." Then she rose up and began tugging at her nightgown.

He helped her. How could he not? It allowed him to stroke her skin, to see the slow reveal of her legs, her honey, and her breasts. Her skin was flawless in the candlelight, and her eyes were luminous as she looked at him.

He wanted to say something. Something that would mark this moment with the wonder he felt, but he had no words. Only the slow appreciation of his gaze, his caress, and his kiss. He pressed his mouth to hers, opening her up, and smiling when she was as enthusiastic as he. Then when she tugged at his shirt, he let his lips trail across her neck and down to her breasts. He would not stop kissing her even to unbutton and remove his shirt. He did that while his lips nipped at her tender nipples.

Her hands found him after his shirt fell away. Her frantic fingers stroked over his shoulders and back while he suckled her until she writhed beneath him. And when his hands slipped between her thighs, she grabbed him.

"No," she said in a husky whisper. "I want you in the normal way. I want—"

He kissed her. He knew what she wanted, and he would give it to her. But first, he would enjoy her, and he would be sure that she was ready. When he lifted off her mouth, he whispered against her ear. "I will give you everything," he said. "But you must trust me in this. It is your first time, and I want it to not hurt."

She nodded, and there was fear in her eyes. Every maiden worried about the first pain.

"Trust me."

He took his time preparing her. He stroked between her legs, he thrust his fingers into her to spread her wide, and he even lowered his mouth to lick his fill of her. She moved with wild abandon beneath him, and she grabbed a pillow to press against her mouth. He heard her cries nonetheless as he sucked her woman's place. And best of all, he felt the grip of her thighs around his shoulders as her body arched in pleasure.

She quickened under his tongue, and he drank in her bliss. And as much as he could, he watched her body ripple with every contraction. Such beauty. Such strength. The pillow had fallen off her face, and her lips parted in delight. Her eyes were dazed, and her hair tumbled in wild abandon. He set his chin on her belly and waited as her breathing steadied.

"That is not what I expected," she finally whispered.

"Tell me when you are ready. There will be more."

She smiled then, but her gaze slipped to where her nightrail lay discarded. "There is a French letter in the pocket."

His brows rose. What did she know of condoms?

"The upstairs ladies gave it to me when I turned twenty-one."

He frowned. "That was four years ago. I'm sorry, Amber, but I don't think the condom will still be good."

Her eyes widened. "But—"

He shook his head. "I have one."

She raised her brows, and he shrugged. "Shall I say that Lord Morthan has them? I found them in the drawer." He opened the nightstand and pulled out a French letter. "I believe this is his way of keeping his son from fathering a bastard."

She nodded and began to straighten up off the bed to watch what he did. He shucked the rest of his clothing in swift motions, and when his cock sprang free, she reached for it. "May I?" she asked.

He didn't know what she wanted, but he could refuse her nothing. So, when she tentatively stroked him and reached for the condom, he let her. His body was thrumming by the time she was finished touching him. And then his hands shook as he taught her how to put the preventive on him.

Soon he was kissing her again. The thrust of his tongue was forceful, as was the way he stroked her breasts. He feared he would hurt her, so he eased his touch, but she gripped his wrists and pulled herself up enough to meet him nose to nose.

"Now," she rasped. "Please, Elliott. Now."

He nodded while gratitude overflowed from his heart. He settled himself between her thighs and slowly pushed forward.

She gasped in surprise, but she didn't move away. In fact, she stretched her legs wider.

"You could never hurt me," she whispered. "I have chosen this. I have chosen you."

Sweet heaven, she was amazing. He pushed in deeper. She arched as she surrounded him in wet heat. And when her heels gripped the back of his thighs, he couldn't hold back any longer.

He thrust inside and felt her maidenhead give way. He heard her gasp as her head arched back, and her fingers gripped his shoulders hard. He stilled. Of course, he stopped. She needed the time, so he waited, not even fully seated. He held himself frozen until he felt her relax. Her breath deepened, and her legs softened around him.

"Amber?"

"There is more, yes?"

"Yes."

He thrust until he was fully inside. She moaned, but this time, not in pain. This time her lips curved in delight. A few moments later, he began to move. The slide of her body around his was like heaven. The smile on her lips as he thrust was incredible. And then she met him with his next pump. She arched into his movement and cried out in delight.

It was like a dam broke inside him. All the passion he held back, all the restraint that had been burned into him since childhood, gave way. He spread her legs wider and thrust deep, claiming her with every movement. He buried himself and jerked against her. He rammed inside and rolled his hips. It was all he could do for her in this maelstrom of need. Everything he knew to bring her to completion again before he lost himself in his own delight.

Her body gripped him. A hot rhythm of hunger that milked him. He gave her everything. He spilled his seed, pouring into her as he steeped in wonder. Wave after wave rolled through him and into her. Heaven.

He fell sideways and gathered her into his arms. He barely had breath but managed to kiss her shoulder and the curve of her neck. She stroked his back and into his hair.

And in that moment, as they touched each other, he knew he had lost his heart to her. She was the woman he loved. The woman for him always. And no matter where country and duty took him, she would be the one to whom he returned.

"I love you," he whispered.

"I love you," she answered.

They held each other late into the night.

When the storm stopped and the clouds parted enough to show the rosy glow of dawn, he roused himself. He scooped her up in his arms and carried her to her bedroom.

He would not disgrace her yet. He would not own her as his mistress yet. That would come soon. For now, he would try to keep her honor intact. So, he kissed her one last time and crept back into the anonymity of his own bedchamber, where he sat and planned for the future.

CHAPTER TWENTY

AMBER RELISHED THE trip home. It wasn't just the warm looks that kept passing between her and Elliott. She realized that soon she would have a home of her own. After all, she couldn't be Elliott's mistress and still live with her father and grandfather. Where would it be? How would it work?

A few of the upstairs ladies had gone this route. It was considered a grand achievement, and many of the girls talked incessantly about what they'd do once it happened for them. She would have plenty of ready advice back at the Lyon's Den, but that was nothing compared to the practical know-how that came from Mrs. Hopkins.

The good housekeeper thought she was asking about her married future with Mr. Jupp. It didn't matter. Maintaining a household was the same, whether for a wife or a mistress. So Amber asked, and Mrs. Hopkins gave good advice, and their discussion made the time pass quickly. As did the sweet way Elliott kept looking at her. Sort of like a bewitched boy but with a man's hunger sparking the depths of his eyes. It warmed her deep inside. And she was sure she gave him equally delighted looks back.

Sadly, her mood changed once they arrived at Diana's home.

There were things to do and people to apprise of her decision. While Mrs. Hopkins hurried downstairs, Elliott leaned down to whisper in her ear, and Amber felt a tingle rush down her spine in excitement for the words he was about to say.

"How soon can the brooch be completed?"

Well, that was not what she'd expected. She'd been hoping he'd say, "I love you," again. But Elliott was a practical man and not prone to sweet words. She'd known that from the beginning. "A day," she answered.

"Can your father do the metalwork without you?"

"Yes."

He made a satisfied sound. "I'll take the wax directly to him. And then I can force the vote tomorrow afternoon."

She smiled, seeing the way the sunlight gleamed in his hair and that his eyes shone bright. But he wasn't looking at her. His thoughts were on the schedule of his day.

"I missed this morning's meeting with Mr. Jupp, but maybe that's for the best." He focused on her. "Can you send him a missive informing him that you two will not suit?"

She nodded. "I will tell him that my heart lies elsewhere."

His brows pulled together in a slight frown. "That may not be the best way. Hearts don't factor into a society marriage."

Her mouth twisted into a grimace. Marriage in the upper crust sounded like a jail sentence. She was choosing the right path. "I will say that we will not suit one another."

"That's better," he said with a nod. "And then I'll send round my apologies and indicate that your choices have taken you elsewhere."

She looked up, hoping that now she would feel the warmth of his gaze. And even though he could not kiss her in the open, she would feel it in a quick caress of his hand or something like that. But he didn't. Instead, his thoughts had jumped elsewhere.

"Where will you be? Do you stay with my sister?"

She disliked lying to a woman who had become a friend. And she would not stay here if it might damage Diana's reputation for housing a courtesan. "I will go home. You can find me in the Lyon's Den."

His face tightened. "I do not like you in that place. Where will you sleep?"

"There are extra beds above the main den. The upstairs girls all sleep separately from where they work." Then she sighed. "Plus, I have to tell my father."

His eyes widened in alarm. "Your father—" His expression tightened as he realized he, too, would have to face the consequences. Her father would not be pleased. In truth, the idea of explaining this to him horrified her. He was not likely to understand, but it had to be done. Her family was too important to her.

"How angry will he be?"

She looked down. "Very. But I will handle it."

"Will he destroy the brooch in anger?"

Maybe. "If he does, I will refashion it."

Elliott looked grim, but he nodded. "I could take you there now. We could do this together."

It was sweet that he wanted to spare her. "I cannot go there immediately. I must make my goodbyes to your sister."

His eyes narrowed a moment, not in anger, but in discernment. "You are going to tell her as well."

She nodded. If they were to do this—become master and mistress—then the people they loved should know.

He shook his head. "That is not the way this is usually done."

"I have always forged my own path."

He exhaled. "Perhaps I should talk to Diana first."

Since he had not touched her, she squeezed his arm. "No. Go get the brooch started so you can get the votes you need. That is more important."

He nodded slowly. For a moment, she thought he'd tell her she was the most important, but that was not what her practical lover would say. His resolution was uppermost in his thoughts, and she would not interfere with what he valued.

"We will speak soon," she said.

He focused on her. His eyes grew more blue than green, and his expression relaxed. "You understand me," he said quietly. "You cannot know how rare that is, especially in a woman."

It wasn't quite a protestation of love, but it was close enough. It warmed her and gave her the strength to face the rest of the day. She stepped back with a smile. He gave her a quick bow before turning back to his carriage and jumping up beside his coachman. Amber had a moment to enjoy his muscular frame and the easy way he leaped onto the bench. Then they were moving away, and she had to go inside to find Diana.

Elliott's sister was with her husband. Amber could hear her voice as she read to the bedridden man. She stood outside the door for a long moment, undecided as to whether she should interrupt or not. But then Diana's voice stopped, and all was quiet. And in that moment, Amber scratched on the door.

There was no verbal response, but in a moment, Diana opened the door. She looked tired, and the scents coming from inside were terrible. Stagnant air and decay not covered by the scented candles that burned in the room. And then Amber got a peek at the shriveled man on the bed. He might once have been a powerful figure, but now he appeared only bones in a body that hissed as he breathed.

"Amber! How wonderful that you are back," Diana said as she stepped outside and closed the door behind her. "I was so worried with the storm."

"It was terrible, but we managed," she answered, her gaze still on the now-closed bedroom door. "I am so sorry," she said. The sickness inside must be terrible to witness.

Diana nodded. "Geoffrey came for a visit last night and upset his father. Today, as usual, things are worse for my husband."

"And you? How did you fare?" She was well aware that one of the reasons for her to stay here was to help protect Diana from her stepson.

"I was away, thank God, but that means I was unable to protect my husband."

It was a husband's job to protect his wife and a son's job not to terrify either father or stepmother, but in this, Diana had not married well. Amber squeezed her hands. "I have something to tell you," she said quietly. "Something that you will not approve."

Diana sighed as she looked at Amber. "The prince has turned your head, hasn't he?"

"The prince?"

"My brother. That's what my mother and I used to call him. Elliott was imperious even as a boy." Diana took her hand, and together they walked into Amber's bedchamber.

Inside, Amber smiled. It appeared she was to have a prince after all. "Of course, he was." Once they were in her bedroom with the door closed, Amber confessed it all. "I have decided to be his mistress. It is the best place for a girl like me. I can still sculpt jewelry. I will have a home of my own, and I love him."

Diana looked at her sadly. "What about children? With Mr. Jupp, your son will be a baron one day."

Amber shook her head, and though the words hurt, she answered with certainty. "I will not have any. I had to choose between love and children, Diana. Please understand that this is what I want."

Diana's expression grew pale and vulnerable. As if she were thinking back on her own life and choices. In the end, she gave a quiet laugh. "I am the last person to criticize you. I can tell you that a respectable marriage has not helped me at all."

No, it had not. "Is there anything I can do?" Amber asked.

Diana looked away as she wiped at her tears. "Be happy. Make my brother happy." Then from down the hallway, they both heard the sound of coughing. Her husband was awake, and Diana straightened up. "I will tell everyone that you have chosen to go back home to see your grandmother."

"Thank you, Diana," Amber stood and gave her an impetuous hug. And as she did, she whispered in her ear. "Beware of Geoffrey. He gambles a great deal at the Lyon's Den. He will only get more desperate as time goes on."

Diana swallowed. "I know." Then after a last melancholy smile, Diana left the bedroom to disappear into the sickroom. She was trapped, and Amber ached for her, but there was nothing to do about it but discuss the matter with Elliott when she could.

For now, there was another person she had to tell, and she doubted that her father would take it nearly as well. She hailed a hackney and went straight to the Lyon's Den. She walked into the shop to meet the glowering stare of her father, who was not making the brooch. In fact, he was not doing anything but sitting and brooding with an underlying simmer of fury.

He knew.

Of course, her father knew. Elliott was not a man to leave that difficult discussion to her. He must have told him when he'd come with the wax carving. And now, what was she to say?

"I love him, Papa. How many times have you told me of the love between you and Mama? How many things would you have given up to be with her? I shall be independent. I shall still carve wax and make jewelry. I can be independent and be with the man I love."

"He should marry you!" her father snapped.

"He cannot. You know that as well as I."

Her father did. They both knew the ways of the aristocracy. And yet, the pain in his eyes when he looked at her tore at her heart. "Your mother would not approve."

That was a stab to her heart. Enough that she flinched. But she lifted her head and spoke the truth. "Then it is good that she is not here to stop me."

"I forbid it!" he roared.

This she had anticipated. "Papa, if you deny me, I will leave today. You will never see me again, and I will carve wax for someone else."

He reared back as if struck because she had indeed hit him where he was most vulnerable. "You wouldn't."

"I would, Papa. Because I am a grown woman, and it is time I left the Lyon's Den."

That was all she would say. So, she passed by him, her body stiff and her arms aching to hug her father. But she didn't. She went into the workshop. She did what was needed to make the brooch. She handled the hot metals and the fire. And after an hour's labor, her father joined her. He didn't say a word. Disapproval radiated off of him, but he helped her fashion the piece. And they did not speak of her future again.

She missed Elliott when he came to pick up the brooch the next day. She was with her grandfather in the cage, and Elliott did not linger in the shop. Whatever words were said between him and her father remained a secret. And though it irked her that he had not stopped to say hello, she understood that a mistress's job was to wait on the man. He did not owe her a visit, and more importantly, she heard from her father that his vote was scheduled for that afternoon.

At least she had time to say her goodbyes to her friends at the Lyon's Den. Many cried. Most applauded her. And as one, the entire establishment waited for the moment Elliott came to claim her for her happily ever after.

He did not show that evening, though she heard from the gossip in the Den that the vote went his way. And she waited through another day.

The next morning, Amber listened to gossip from the ladies' side about Lady Morthan's granddaughter. Apparently, the girl had worn the brooch during her presentation to the Prince Regent, and all was well there. An excellent outcome, at least for now. Her grandson was still a thief who should never gamble.

Mr. Christopher Jupp visited the shop on the third day of waiting. They spoke quickly and quietly, and she told him the truth. She was in love with someone else and could not go against her heart. She was not meant for society, and so she would stay here and make jewelry in secret. And when their conversation was over, she passed him a list of women she thought would please him better. She had met a few who were not spiteful. Ones who might understand his artistic soul.

And she waited through another day and night.

By the fourth day, the women in the Lyon's Den were giving her pitying looks. As many stories as there were of women who became mistresses, there were five times that number of girls being tricked by a man's promise. Of women who languished in wait because the man they trusted had lied.

But that wouldn't happen to her. She knew Elliott. He was simply busy. He was arranging things. He would not abandon her because he loved her. Hadn't he said so on the night she had given him her virginity?

He loved her.

Or perhaps he had gotten what he wanted and now had disappeared when it came time to pay for what she wanted. A home of her own was expensive. Perhaps with distance, he had realized she wasn't that special after all. Perhaps his mother had found the perfect wife for him, and he was busy courting that paragon.

Such fears ran through her mind. She dismissed them as best she could. Elliott would come for her. She only had to wait a little longer.

On the fifth day, Mrs. Dove-Lyon invited her to tea. Amber went and listened for an entire hour to stories of women who had been fooled by clever men. Amber was not alone, declared the den owner. Many a girl—Mrs. Dove-Lyon included—had come out stronger and smarter after being swindled. The woman meant well, but her words did not help Amber. Elliott would come for her. She declared it loudly and believed it with all her heart. It was only her mind that disagreed.

It didn't help that the weather continued to be abominable. Drizzle at the beginning of the week, storms in the middle, and now more rain, such as must have been seen by Noah in his ark. Anyone who ventured outside became drenched in what felt like the displeasure of an angry god. Everyone's mood was terrible because no one liked hunkering down in their homes. Those that ventured out were soaked to the skin and terrified of illness.

And still, Amber waited while her father paced and glowered at the sky. No customers came in such weather and no Elliott either. Until the night when the sky was pitch black, the roads were more water than mud, and someone banged hard on the den door.

Amber was bringing her grandfather tea in the cage. If she had been locked inside, she would not have heard the prodigious male sneeze that accompanied the gust of bitter wind that blew in from the open door. But she was heading back upstairs, and so she did hear it, and she heard a voice, too. A male voice, dominant and filled with irritation. "Where is Amber Gohar? Or Thisbe Gold?"

Elliott!

He was here! On a night fit for only the devil, Elliott had finally come.

"Wherever she is," grumbled Lysander from the door. "She ain't willing to see you."

"Yes, I am!" she cried as she started to rush forward. But she was holding her grandfather's tea and sloshed it as she moved. Cursing, she handed the tray to the nearest person—many had looked up at the noise, and she rushed forward. Fortunately, she didn't have to go far. Elliott was mounting the steps three at a time, and they came face to face at the top.

"Amber," he breathed as he brushed water out of his eyes.

"Elliott!" she said as she stepped back a bit from the wet splash of his clothes. "You're soaked through."

"I am. It's beastly out there, but I was tired of waiting. Though I fear my horse will never forgive me."

What was she to say to that? He was standing there looking large and half-drowned while talking about his horse. She wanted to touch him. She wanted to wrap him in dry things before he fell ill. But it had been six long days without word from him. What was she supposed to think?

"I meant to send a message, but everything went crazy. Gwen is in trouble."

"Oh no!"

"It's all right for now, but I couldn't get away to see you. Not when she was in such a state."

"And your resolution passed."

He frowned as if he were just remembering it. "Oh, yes. It did." He rubbed the water off his face with a self-conscious laugh. "That was so important to me, but I barely remember it now."

Really? She had no idea what to say about that. "But your sister is well now?"

"Yes. She brought it on herself. That's Gwen through and through. And the whole time, I wanted to talk with you about it. I wanted to know what you thought and if you knew what could be done to help. If...any of a thousand things."

"I was right here." She couldn't keep the note of accusation out of her voice. She'd been waiting for him.

"I know. I know. But..." He took her hands in his icy ones. "I needed to think. I needed to..." He shrugged. "I went to another of those horrible Almack's evenings."

So he had been looking for a wife. She had guessed as much. Indeed, she knew she would always come in second to the woman he eventually married. But it hurt to know she had been waiting on him, that she had defended him to all those people who said he had betrayed her, and all the while, he had been looking for his wife.

Tears sprang to her eyes, and she tried to move away. She didn't want him to see her cry. Not when she chose this. Not when she'd known all along and yet, still the ache in her chest was too much. The pain of holding back her tears burned like fire in her throat.

"I couldn't do it, Amber. I hated looking at them. They are nothing like you, and I couldn't stand the idea of marrying a single one."

It took a moment for his words to penetrate her fight to hold in her tears. But when she finally repeated his words in her head, she blinked and frowned at him. "But you will have to marry one of them eventually." The words came out in an anguished whisper, but he heard her nonetheless.

"That's what my mother said, but it's not true. It's not." He tugged her closer to him, and she took a stumbling step forward. "If I want to lead the government as Prime Minister, then yes, I would have to marry one of them."

"But you do want that."

He shook his head. "I did want that. But Amber, I want you more."

Her breath choked off. He wanted her. He loved her. The tears spilled from her eyes, and she pushed forward despite his wet state. He stopped her, holding her back until she looked at him in surprise. "Elliott?"

"You don't understand. I don't want those other ladies as a wife. I want you."

"Yes, you said that."

"I hate the idea of not being able to see you whenever I want, of not having you by my side for everything. For when my mother has one of her problems, for when Gwen gets into trouble. And that doesn't even begin to address Diana or Lilah."

"I will do whatever I can. You know that."

"Yes, I do. Which is why I had to leave in this beastly weather."

"What?"

"I had to ride all the way to Kent to the family estate. It's a mess, I tell you. I'm doing everything I can there, and you'll hate it if you ever go there."

"I won't," she whispered. She wouldn't ever go there. A mistress never went to the family estate.

"You will, mark my words. You will. But that is something else that I wish to speak to you about, though it is horrible far away. And in the rain, I couldn't go more than thirty miles without stopping. That's why I took so long."

His words were so scattered that she began to fear for his health. Normally, he spoke with clear and direct purpose, but he was rushing his words, and they made little sense.

"Elliott, are you ill? Do you have a fever?" She put her hand to his cheek and felt the wet heat there. Not so much that he seemed feverish, but it was hard to tell. Especially as he grabbed her hand and pressed a kiss to her palm.

"Amber, my darling, I cannot—I will not—live without you." And then he began to sink. His legs must have given out because he dropped down to the floor before her. She cried out in alarm, but he kept sinking, and he was too large for her to hold.

It took her a long moment to realize that he hadn't collapsed. He was, in fact, on one knee before her. Behind her, she heard men and women gasp in surprise, but she didn't understand what was happening. What was he doing—

He pulled a ring out of his pocket. It was old, made of heavy gold, and bore the Byrn family crest on it. "I know this is ugly," he said. "Nothing like the things you make, but it is traditional. It is what every Byrn countess has worn on her wedding day."

She blinked at it, her thoughts frozen as she stared. She saw the age of the ring and the craftsmanship, which was a ridiculous thing to look at. Not when he was on one knee and holding it out to her. But he had said from the very beginning, over and over, that he could not marry her. So what was he doing now?

"Please, Amber Gohar. Please do me the greatest honor and become my wife."

Behind her, everyone exclaimed. But Amber just stared at Elliott on his knee before her, ring outstretched. "You cannot mean that," she whispered. "I have already given you my heart. You don't need to ruin yourself for me."

He grabbed her hand. "I am not ruining myself. Amber, you are the making of me. Look." He pulled back his coat and showed her his waistcoat. It was black, and she stared at it in confusion.

"I don't understand," she whispered.

"Oh, blast," he grumbled. "It's got colors in it. You can't see it now, but there's red in there. I swear!"

Someone obligingly brought a lamp forward, and sure enough, there were threads of dark red in it. "It's...beautiful?" she said. It wasn't really. It was wet and wrinkled.

"I'll get another one. You pick the colors, even if it's yellow. I'm not partial to yellow, you see, but I will for you. If you say it's beautiful, I will wear it." He grabbed her hand again and looked in her eyes. "I love you, Amber. Please say you will be my countess. Please."

Her breath choked off, and her eyes widened. It was happening. Everything was coming true. Not only did she have a prince, but he was proposing to her on the ugliest night of the year. Soaking wet, shivering with cold, and all because he had to get her the family ring.

"You have swept me off my feet," she murmured.

"Not yet, I haven't. But I will if you don't mind getting wet."

"I don't mind," she said. "I seem to have fallen desperately in love with you."

He pressed the ring forward. "Then say yes, Amber. Yes, you will marry me."

"Yes! Of course, yes!" she said as she fumbled to put on the ring. He helped her. And then, just like he'd promised, he swept her up in his arms. And while everyone cheered, he kissed her. Hard and hot, then sweet and happy. They clung to each other, and she pressed herself against him and wrapped her arms around his broad shoulders.

"Do you know what?" she whispered into his ear.

"What, my heart?"

"We are going to live happily ever after, and it's going to be wonderful!"

"Yes, my love. Yes, it will."

"And I'm going to wear my bracelet, Elliott. On my wedding day, I'm going to wear the one with a firebird surrounded in flames."

"A bird in flight. So long as you always fly back to me."

She pressed her face to his neck. She hung on to him and kissed his throat, his jaw, and then his mouth. And when they were finished, she whispered her answer. "I'll always fly back to you. Because I love you."

"And you're my happily ever after. The one I didn't even know I was missing."

Epilogue

IF ANYONE HAD told the child Amber how much work was involved in a society wedding, she would likely have created other dreams. But she'd had not one inkling of what was involved until she was up to her neck in plans. Elliott's entire family was recruited, as was her own. Even Mrs. Dove-Lyon lent a hand to make her and Elliott's wedding the society event of the year. And though many a stiff-minded matron refused the invitation, many more were bribed into the event.

Every single woman in attendance received a silver pin fashioned by Amber's hand. The expense was excessive, but the result well worth the effort. Amber's true identity was not only acknowledged but celebrated, as was her art. And if the *ton* responded with greed, then the price was accepting Amber into their midst. And they did so with enthusiasm.

The plan was hatched by Elliott's mother. The expense was born by Amber's father with an advance from Mrs. Dove-Lyon. And somehow, Elliott got the Prince Regent to make an appearance at the wedding breakfast.

The prince ate a meal with them, and Amber was so overwhelmed that Mrs. Hopkins had to bring her a special cup of tea to get her stomach to settle.

Amber didn't drink it. Instead, she held her husband's hand and smiled as he whispered three words into her ear.

"Happily, ever after."

She laughed. "I thought you were going to say you love me."

"I do. Always. Forever. I cannot believe you are finally my wife."

And Amber couldn't believe that the idea of spending the rest of her life with Elliott was more amazing to her than the fact that the Prince Regent promised to dance with her at the very next opportunity.

So she pressed a kiss to her husband's cheek and whispered into his ear. "I don't know what to do," she said. "It's terrible."

He jerked back, his eyes darting about as he searched the room, no doubt, for a dragon to slay. "What has happened? What can I do?"

"I am so happy. I have nothing left to dream about. What can I hope for if everything is exactly as I want?"

"Children? Passage of my next resolution? A truly excellent breakfast buffet?"

"Yes, yes, all of those. But…" How could she put her question into words? It wasn't even clear in her own head. It wasn't until she saw her father surreptitiously wiping away a tear that she knew the answer to what she wanted next. "I shall dream of everyone else becoming as happy as I am. Of finding their true love just as we have."

"I like that dream," Elliott said as he pressed a kiss to her lips.

"I love you," she said when she had the breath to respond.

"Not nearly as much as I love you," he answered.

And then, with a giddy smile, she turned her attention to finding a solution for Diana.

About the Author

JADE LEE has two passions (well, except for her family, but that's a given). She loves dreaming up stories and playing racquetball, not always in that order. When her pro-racquetball career ended with a pair of very bad knees, she turned her attention to writing. An author of more than 30 romance novels, she's decided that life can be full of joy without ever getting up from her chair.

A USA Today Bestseller, Jade has been scripting love stories since she first picked up a set of paper dolls. Ball gowns and rakish lords caught her attention early (thank you Georgette Heyer), and her fascination with the Regency began. She's just embarked on a new Regency series, RAKES AND ROGUES. Her love of romance extends to the present day, too.

So if you love that special feeling when two people just fit, then contact her through her website www.JadeLeeAuthor.com or www.KathyLyons.com.

CPSIA information can be obtained
at www.ICGtesting.com
Printed in the USA
LVHW081536130320
649997LV00008B/430